A. FRANK SMITH, JR. LIBRARY CENTER
SOUTHWESTERN UNIVERSIT
GEORGETOWN, TEXAS 786

P9-AQM-361

WITHDRAWN

A. FRANK SMITH, JR. LIBRARY CENTER
SOUTHWESTERN UNIVERSITY

3 3053 00245 0344

CF B886s

Bunting, Eve, 1928-

Someone is hiding on
 Alcatraz Island

SOMEONE IS HIDING ON ALCATRAZ ISLAND

SOMEONE IS HIDING ON ALCATRAZ ISLAND

Eve Bunting

CLARION BOOKS

TICKNOR & FIELDS: A HOUGHTON MIFFLIN COMPANY

NEW YORK

Clarion Books
Ticknor & Fields, a Houghton Mifflin Company
Copyright © 1984 by Eve Bunting

All rights reserved. No part of this book may be reproduced or transmitted in any form or by any means, electronic or mechanical, including photocopying and recording, or by any information storage or retrieval system, except as may be expressly permitted by the 1976 Copyright Act or in writing by the publisher. Requests for permission should be addressed in writing to Clarion Books, 52 Vanderbilt Avenue, New York, NY 10017.

Printed in the U.S.A.

Library of Congress Cataloging in Publication Data

Bunting, Eve, 1928–
　Someone is hiding on Alcatraz Island.

　Summary: When he offends the toughest gang in his San Francisco school, Danny tries to elude them by going to Alcatraz only to find himself and a Park Service employee trapped by the gang in an old prison cell block.

　[1. Gangs — Fiction. 2. Alcatraz Island, Calif. — Fiction] I. Title.
PZ7.B91527Sn 1984　　[Fic]　　84-5019
ISBN 0-89919-219-X

P 10 9 8 7 6

CF
B886a

For Sloan
who shares my interest in Alcatraz

CHAPTER

1

I suddenly saw the four of them, standing around the Human Jukebox. They were only a half a block away from me, but they hadn't seen me. I could still run. I could still get away. But any second now, one of them would look up — Cowboy or one of the other Outlaws — Maxie probably, because he was never still, his head always bobbing and his eyes tracking this way and that, looking for who was out to get him. Or more likely, for who he was out to get. Like me. Just because I'd done that one stupid thing. If only I could turn time back to when the Outlaws didn't know I existed.

Maxie was peering in the slot where the Human Jukebox's customers dropped the money for the tunes Human played for them. But any second now ... any second....

I tried to breathe deeply and not panic. Step back ... don't turn ... it's never wise to turn your back on the Outlaws. Maxie had moved from the Jukebox and was staring over the bay. He held his big, black radio close to his ear. Maxie always carried that gigantic, black box. His legs jiggled in time to whatever he heard, and his face had this stupid smile on it.

The usual tourist swarm on Fisherman's Wharf pushed around me. Plenty of people. People to hide me. A fat guy in a blue duffle coat was between me and the Outlaws, and I leaped back, right into a trestle table piled high with wooden flutes. The cardboard sign on the table wobbled and began to fall. INTERGALACTIC CHURCH OF GOD, it said. SUPPORT OUR CAUSE.

"Hey! You! Watch it!" The guy behind the table had long hair and a headband. He was grabbing for the sign, and it was me he was bellowing at.

The flutes slid off the table, rattling and clattering onto the ground. Who would have thought a bunch of rolling flutes could make this much noise? I tried to catch them, looked up, and saw Maxie's eyes jumping all over me. Oh no! Oh please!

2

He pointed, and Cowboy and Priest and Jelly Bean turned in my direction.

I dropped the flutes that had tumbled into my arms and began running. Behind me the guy from the Intergalactic Church of God screamed words that didn't sound very holy.

I was running hard, my breath hot in my throat. Running is the thing I do best. I was creaming past Francisco's and the Alioto Fish Company. The wind from the bay whipped the faded flags, making a snapping sound. Running through fish smells, through old ropey smells. Running, running. Tourists stopped to stare, to point, licking at ice-cream cones, spooning shrimp cocktail from dripping paper cups. Feet behind me, pounding.

"Rud Daddy! Rud! Rud!" Jelly Bean's voice always sounds as if he has a stuffed up nose. My name is Danny, not Daddy. And he didn't need to tell me to run. I was running. But where? Where was there to run that they couldn't get me?

The fishing boats nosed the docks. A guy hosing the deck of one of them lifted his head to watch, and the stream of water rose and splashed over my tennis shoes. Past the wax museum and Ripley's Believe It Or Not. Where to run? They were going to corner me. Maxie would have his switchblade, and Jelly Bean the big, old buck knife he kept in a sheath on his belt. Priest would have his ice pick, the one he used to clean his nails. I turned my head. They were coming, Cowboy in front, his long legs eating up the space between us. I can run faster than fast, but his legs are twice as long as mine. They'd get me. They'd get me for sure.

The Balclutha, the big sailing ship, towered over me. A museum. I could run in there, maybe find a place to hide. There'd be guards. They always had guards in places like that. I'd tell them what was happening. They wouldn't let Maxie get me. I had money in my jeans. I fished for it, trying not to slow down. A dollar to get on. Maybe Cowboy and the others wouldn't have a dollar. They wouldn't be allowed on. Who was I kidding? Who would stop them? Not some guy in a sailor cap standing at the bottom of a gangplank. Cowboy would give one shove, and the guy would be only a splash in the water.

I raced along the pier, not tiring, but losing ground, and then I saw it . . . the boat for Alcatraz.

The big motor cruiser was loaded to the gills for the trip to the island. Its motors began revving up. The dock men threw off the ropes. I thought about Cowboy's legs scissoring away the distance between us. Desperation gave me extra speed. Two fifty for a ticket. No time to pay, though. I pelted past the ticket booth, down the ramp.

"Hey!" A guy in a blue uniform put out his arm to grab me. I slipped away from him.

"Where's your ticket?" he bellowed. I threw three bucks on the ground at his feet. The wind blew one past him and he stretched for it. "No time," I screamed back. "Gotta get ... on board."

"You can't ..." he began, but the wind took the rest of his sentence and tossed it away. I jumped. The distance between the boat and the dock was ·vider than I'd thought. My feet just made it, finding a toehold on the wooden deck outside the railing. My hands scrabbled too, clutching at the rail. I climbed over and was aboard.

The guy was shouting something else now, but the roar of the motors picking up speed drowned him out.

"What do you think you're doing, kid?" an old man in a Giants cap asked. "You coulda got yourself killed."

No kidding, I thought. I looked back at Cowboy, who had stopped halfway down the ramp. The wind swept his hair back under his big western hat. He could have been Clint Eastwood standing there in his blue jeans and his checked shirt and his tooled leather boots. Cowboy didn't yell or do anything. He just stood, watching, as the boat pulled out. Cowboy is a real quiet guy. But when he speaks, people listen.

Maxie and Jelly Bean were crowding Cowboy now, and even over the engine noise and the distance of water, I could hear Jelly Bean's scream.

"Just wait, Daddy-Boy. You gotta cub back."

Fat little Priest was still puffing along up by the Balclutha. There was a lot of safety now between me and the Outlaws, and my heart started to slow. Free! I was free!

I turned to look at the bridge stretching from the city to the misty beauty of Marin. Clouds hung low in the sky. A sailboat tacked across the bay's choppy waters, its canvas flapping in the wind. There was always wind here, wind and fog and cold. I shivered.

The sweat on me had dried to ice and my T-shirt leeched to me, wet and clammy. Ugh. I'd better get inside, out of the wind. The boat lurched and its nose turned toward Alcatraz. I looked where the boat pointed. The old prison sat big and square at the top of the island. Near it stood a lighthouse. At the right, the trees grew thick and lush down to the wrinkled bottle green of the bay.

Alcatraz isn't a prison anymore. The whole island is a national park with guided tours and boats that run every hour or so. I've never been there; in fact, I've never wanted to go. Maybe that's because of my father. But I was going now.

I turned to look back once at San Francisco. Coit Tower stuck up like a cigar against the sky. I could still see the old yellow arch of Pier 43, but if the Outlaws were waiting for me in front of it, distance had made them disappear. I wished it would make them disappear forever. A seagull drifted behind our boat calling its high, angry cry, and I remembered Jelly Bean. "You gotta cub back, Daddy-Boy. You gotta cub back."

CHAPTER

2

It was just three days ago that I made my fatal mistake. I'm not the kind of guy who looks for trouble, in fact I look the other way. To stay alive in Jefferson High, it's best to do that, and to mind your own business, especially if you're fourteen and small for your age, which I am. It's best to stay clear of jerks like the Outlaws, or the Bear Claws, the other bunch of toads in school, or even the ChiChis, the girl gang that's every bit as mean as the other two.

So why did I do what I did three days ago, right at the start of spring vacation? Well, for one thing, I hadn't any idea that the guy who mugged the old lady was Priest's kid brother. I didn't even know he

8

had a kid brother. Who'd think Priest and the rest of the Outlaws would have mothers and brothers and stuff, like normal people?

I realized later that the guy did look like Priest. But plenty of guys are porky and wear glasses and have a faceful of zits. How was I supposed to make the connection? For another thing, the old lady reminded me of my grandmother who lives with us. She was wearing the kind of sweater that's so old it rises up in the back, and when she screamed I was right next to her. The guy had thrown her down real hard on the sidewalk, and for a minute I was mad as a bull.

So I chased him. And since I run pretty good I caught him and I knocked him down and sat on his fat belly, and when he looked up at me and wheezed, "You turkey! You'll be sorry, I'll tell my brother and he'll get you," I just bounced harder on his belly and grinned.

"Turkey yourself," I said cheerfully. "Think I'm scared of your big brother, Bloato?" and I squeezed his stomach even harder. When he tried to get up, his glasses fell off and I accidentally squashed them with my elbow. Who would have guessed his big brother was Priest?

There was another reason I chased the guy, of course. I chased him because he was small as me — fat and soft and unfit, and catchable. If he'd been a big, mean-looking guy like Maxie or Cowboy or

Jelly Bean, I never would have gone after him, not if the old lady really had been my grandmother. I gave my name to the cops when they came, right out loud where fat boy could hear me, and I felt like a hero. I'm not feeling much like a hero now.

There was a woman with crutches sitting with her back to the boat's railing.

"Excuse me," I asked her. "Do you know how long the Alcatraz tour lasts?"

"About two hours." One of her crutches slid a little and she pulled it back beside her. "I hope I can handle it. It was probably silly of me to come. But I'm leaving tomorrow. And you can't be in San Francisco without seeing Alcatraz!"

Not if you're a tourist, I thought. Two hours! Two hours and then I'd have to come back. But I had time to figure something out. Whatever I figured had better be good.

I pushed inside the boat and down the steps into the warmth and the noise. The concession stand was jammed with customers. Little kids ran up and down the aisles. People sipped coffee and soft drinks at the small Formica tables. There was no place to sit. I leaned against the wall, staring out of the spray-washed windows. I was still shivering. Maybe I should get myself some coffee.

There was a girl sitting on one of the benches. I looked down, and she returned my glance and smiled. She was probably nineteen or so. She was wearing khaki pants and a green jacket with a National Parks patch on the arm. Bright red hair curled out from under one of those big Smokey Bear hats. I'd always thought the only girls who had heart-shaped faces were in dumb old songs, the kind my grandmother likes to sing along with Lawrence Welk on Saturday nights. But that's exactly the kind of face this girl had. She was really beautiful!

I was staring and I felt my face getting hot. I'm not used yet to being fourteen and noticing girls.

"Hi," the girl said. "Aren't you freezing?"

I nodded.

"It'll be worse on the island. It's always twenty degrees colder over there. Especially this late in the day."

I nodded again. That was another thing. I have a hard time talking to girls now. Especially girls like this. Not that I've come across too many like this.

"You want to sit down?" She slid along the plastic bench and made room for me beside her.

I sat down, keeping my arms squeezed tight to my sides. I probably stank with all that dried-out fear and sweat.

I concentrated my thoughts on the Outlaws.

I shouldn't have come to Fisherman's Wharf today. I should have guessed it would be the kind of place the Outlaws would like to hang around. All those big-eyed tourists, just waiting to be plucked. Wallets sticking out of their back pockets, purses left on benches while the women took pictures of their husbands with the Bay Bridge in the background. Easy pickings for the Outlaws.

The thing is, I'm crazy about Fisherman's Wharf. It's so loud and dirty and wonderful. All those smells. The lobsters, boiling in their great bubbling vats. The piled up loaves of sourdough bread. The windows with their tacky shell stuff — houses made out of shells, music boxes made out of shells, big shells made out of little shells.

I like the ride on the rattly cable car, standing on the side, hanging back into the wind. Careening down toward Filbert, expecting all the time that the brakes will give and we'll go roaring on, clanging and clattering into the bay. It's the best roller coaster ride ever.

So today I came. I shouldn't have; If I'd stayed home I'd be safe now. Mom would be at work, and Gran and I would probably be watching one of her game shows on TV. Sure, next week in school I'd have had to face the Outlaws. But I'd worked out a plan. I'd get to school late and sit by the door. I'd jump up the second the bell rang, and I'd run all the way home. I'd stay away from the lockers and out of the bathrooms. Heck, I'd hold it in all day, no sweat. The thing to do was not to drink any juice or milk in the morning. I'd take care never to be by myself, either. I'd stick close to Curt and Willie B, who's pretty big. Not as big as Maxie or Cowboy or

Jelly Bean, but bigger than me. Who isn't? But then, after I'd figured out that great plan, I came down to the wharf and walked right into them.

I tried to think what I should do now. How about if I told this girl? She was a ranger. Wasn't a ranger a kind of a cop? But if I told, it would be worse for me afterwards. It was always worse if you finked on the Outlaws. I remembered Tom Black, who'd told Mr. Carson about Jelly Bean taking his lunch money. Tom was only an eighth grader and didn't know any better. The Outlaws got him in the bathroom. They crammed his two quarters into his mouth, one at a time, and held his nose till he swallowed. Fortunately, as Tom said, "They both came out all right in the end." He meant the quarters. Tom didn't tell about the Outlaws that second time. He probably never told anything about anyone again.

The girl was reading a paperback book. I could see the title, *The Best of Everything*. It had three gorgeous women on the front. One looked a little bit like Miss Rawlings, our art teacher.

"Hi!" A black guy in a ranger uniform had stopped in front of us. "What you reading, Biddy?"

The girl put the book down. "Hi, David. It's an oldie but a goodie."

The guy nodded. "What's the matter with you anyway? Can't you stay away from this place? I thought this was your day off."

"It is."

"Does Maybelline know you're coming?" he asked.

I was listening, trying to look as if I wasn't.

"No," the girl said. "It's Maybelline's birthday. The big 5–0. I'm on in the morning. So I decided to come over early and keep her company. Nobody should face the big 5–0 alone, right? I've got a present for her stashed under her bunk."

David grinned. "The big 5–0, huh? She'd kill if she knew you told! Catch you later, Biddy."

Biddy shouted after him. "If you see Maybelline, don't tell her I'm staying over. It's a secret, okay?"

David looked back over his shoulder. "Okay."

I heard the motors change gears and slow down, and when I turned to look out of the window I saw we were edging around the right side of the island.

People were crowding the aisles now, jamming the stairs, impatient to be off. I thought about the prisoners who must have come out here once by boat, Scarface and people like that. They probably weren't in such a rush to leave the boat and get out onto the Rock.

The girl ranger was standing too, stuffing the book into the pocket of her jacket. She was just about the same height as me which is an okay height for a girl, but shrimpy for a boy. I stretched my spine as far up as it would go. It's something I know how to do, because I do stretching exercises every day. My theory is, if my tendons and things know I mean business, they'll cooperate and stay stretched.

"Hey!" The girl's hand was on my arm, astonishing me. "Come on back here with me. I'll just bet somebody left a jacket on this boat today. You could wear it, and then leave it here when you come back after the tour. It's blowing a gale out there."

"I'm all right, honest," I began. But somehow I was walking behind her, and she was asking the woman at the concession stand if there'd been any coats left today, and the woman was saying, "Sure enough," and pulling stuff from underneath her counter and dumping it on top. There was a mess of coats and umbrellas and scarves and books. The woman pawed through the jackets. "Is one of these his?"

"Uh uh." Biddy picked up a red windbreaker with a heavy lining and a hood. "He's just going to borrow this one for a couple of hours." I could tell straight off it was too big, but I didn't say anything.

Biddy held the jacket while I slipped my arms into the sleeves. I tried to stretch my arms, too.

Biddy nodded. "Terrific."

The woman behind the counter said, "It's an ill wind that blows nobody good. Don't forget to bring it back, son," she added.

I hate to be called son. Especially in front of a girl like Biddy.

"Let's go," Biddy said. "Unless you want to miss

the tour and head straight back to the city?"

That I did not want.

I moved at a fast clip toward the steps and up on the deck. We were the last ones off.

It wasn't quite blowing a gale, but it was coming close. The wind came in gusts and I felt a sprinkle of rain. I pushed my hands deep in the jacket pockets and found a wad of dirty Kleenex, a pair of sunglasses, and one of those little metal nail clippers. I wrapped my fingers around it. I could snitch it and use it as a weapon against the Outlaws when I got back.

Three park rangers were standing on a raised platform just beyond the dock. Everyone crowded around them, giving the guys their full attention. Actually, I saw that one was a black girl, not a guy. To my left was a low wooden hut that was probably the ranger office. Behind it loomed a dirty white building with small windows.

"Is that the prison?" a girl asked a guy who was cuddling her, keeping her safe from the sea breezes. You could tell he was the kind of guy who knew everything.

"No. Those were the old administration buildings. You think they'd put the prison down here, right by the water? Come on! It's way up there on top of the hill."

I stood at the back of the group. Boy, it was cold, even in the red jacket. I turned around to thank

Biddy again, but she was walking away from me, and the black girl ranger was smiling at her, calling her over. The ranger couldn't be Maybelline, the one with the birthday. This one didn't look as if she'd reached the big 2–0. Now Biddy was walking across the dock. Well, that was that. I'd probably never see her again. It would be nice if we'd meet in about four years when I'd be eighteen and she'd be about twenty-three. Age wouldn't matter a darn then. I'd have grown too. I'd be towering over her, and I'd say, "Remember me? We met on the way to Alcatraz."

Four years. If I lived that long.

I looked across the bay at the distant gleam of San Francisco. The sun was shining over there, turning the hills to brilliant green, softening and gilding the city. It looked like paradise. Here it was cold and menacing. Maybe that was the way it was supposed to be when you were in prison. You could see paradise, but you couldn't get to it. I didn't want to get to it myself, not with the Outlaws barring its gate.

I turned up the collar of the jacket and faced the three rangers. One of them raised his voice against the wind. "Welcome to Alcatraz," he said.

CHAPTER

3

They divided us into three groups. I was with a guy with a fringe of beard stuck under his chin. He looked stern. He said his name was Richard, and I'd lay odds he got kidded about being Ranger Rick. I could tell he took his job seriously. I really didn't want to go up to see the prison, but there was no way to stay behind. We were on a tour, and on a tour everyone goes. I saw the lady with the crutches hobbling up close to the front.

Every now and then Ranger Rick would stop, gather us around him, and tell us a bunch of things. I hadn't thought I'd be interested at all, but I was.

It was good stuff. All about how the island had once been a fortress called Fort Alcatraz, then it was a military prison before it became a federal penitentiary. I told myself this wasn't anything like where my father had been held. But then, I didn't know in exactly what kind of place he *had* been held.

The ranger told us that all the worst dudes from the other prisons were sent here to The Rock. My father had been a good guy. But that hadn't made any difference. Ranger Rick was saying how Alcatraz had been escape-proof. I guess my dad's was escape-proof, too. Otherwise he'd have gotten away before they killed him.

We climbed and climbed up the switchback road, past what had been the warden's house, past the chapel that the ranger said had been for the guards, but not the inmates. Facing us on the way up, the second hill was an underground room. There was no door, so we could see inside.

"That was the morgue," the ranger told us. "It used to have a door that was left open. The prisoners could see inside on their first trip up the hill. That way they knew that death was the only way out of Alcatraz." I was trying again not to think about my dad. But out here it wasn't easy.

"Pretty demoralizing," one guy said.

The ranger nodded. "It was meant to be."

I tramped on with the others, my mind skittering around as I tried to come up with a plan to outwit the Outlaws. I couldn't waste time listening to all this informative stuff. I had to think of something. Suppose I did tell the ranger, and asked him for a ranger guard when we got back? Maybe they could circle me and give me safe passage, like Secret Service men with the president.

"Who are these Outlaws?" he'd ask, and I'd say they were the worst four punks in my school. And he'd say, "They're school kids?" And I'd say, "Big ones. Twelfth graders. Maxie must be eighteen. He flunked twice," and the ranger would frown and say, "Come on guy! You gotta learn to fight your own battles."

He'd never believe the Outlaws were as bad as they were. I could try telling him about Bobby Blue, who'd been real good at imitating Jelly Bean's stuffed nose voice. Everybody used to laugh. Bobby doesn't do Jelly Bean anymore. He sticks with John Wayne and R2D2, people like that. He hasn't done Jelly Bean since the day he found all his pigeons with their throats cut. Bobby loved his pigeons. He had a loft for them and coops and everything. He told me there was blood and feathers all over the place. He even brought a dead one out to show us, but I only took a quick look. Its feathers were all black and glued together.

"Jelly Bean's the knife man," I'd said to Curt afterwards. "But it was probably Maxie who did this, with his switchblade. It's delicate work. Pigeon necks are kind of puny."

Curt grinned. "Good thing they don't have a chain man. It'd be pretty messy beating birds to death with a big, old chain."

Sometimes Curt's kind of sick himself. That was disgusting.

"You know what?" I said. "I bet they're glad of an excuse, those guys. Any little insult, any put-down and they're off. It's like a mission."

There'd be no use in my telling the ranger that I was their mission now. No use telling him about the four guys in masks who'd jumped Jerry Cordelli outside his house one night. There were three tall ones and one little fat one. One of the tall ones had a big radio held tight against his ear. The little fat guy stuck an ice pick through Jerry's foot. Jerry hadn't been able to give the police much descrip-tion because of the masks and also because he had passed out. I don't blame him. I'd have passed out the minute they jumped me.

Jerry was in Priest's P.E. class, and he'd kicked him by accident when he was working on the wall bars. Priest screamed that he'd done it on purpose. Priest smiled a lot all the time Jerry was in the hospital. He cleaned his nails a lot too, rolling his ice pick between his thumb and his pudgy fingers.

Of course the main reason Jerry hadn't told was

because then the Outlaws would have really fixed him. They'd have jammed the ice pick through something worse than his foot. Jerry knew that. And I knew that telling the ranger would be the wrong move for me. The Outlaws were mad enough at me already. They'd go berserk if the cops came after them. Jerry Cordelli never did come back to school. Maybe I could get a transfer, too. It would have to be all the way out of California.

We'd walked to the top of the winding road and were in the cell blocks now. Believe me, if I'd thought Alcatraz was a downer before, it was the pits up here. The people huddled around the ranger, talking in whispers. There was nothing to see but cages and more cages, stretching up in tiers to a roof where light filtered in bleakly through more bars. In front of us, the lines of cells marched on either side as far as I could see. The place was enormous. It was like one of the great empty hangars for the military jets that our Boy's Club had seen on a tour of Vandenberg Air Force Base. Somewhere a foghorn groaned. The ranger coughed, and the sound echoed against the emptiness.

"This is Broadway," he said. "The prisoners called the cell blocks after streets in their own towns. It made them feel more at home."

It was supposed to be a joke, I guess, but it was a pretty lame one. A few people laughed. I've discovered though that people laugh to cover up stuff. I do it all the time myself, and I could tell by the faces around me what they really felt. Fear. Too many men had lived here for too many years. The walls and the floors and the dank air had soaked up their despair and held it for all this time.

"Each cell is nine feet by five feet."

I shivered. That's not even as wide as I'm tall. Men had lived in those. Lived their whole lives! I felt the walls closing in on me, and I wasn't even inside. How big had the room, or the cell, or the dungeon been where they'd held my dad? I wished I weren't here. I didn't want to look at these things.

"As you can see," the ranger said, "the cell contains only the bare essentials."

Bare essentials was right. There was a gray toilet, a grimy washbasin, and a metal table and bench, both bolted to the wall. A monkey would feel suffocated in a cage like that. Once there must have been a bed, too . . . a metal cot probably, taking up half of what space there was. But there were no cots now. The walls were crumbling; plaster flaked off onto the floor. It was the kind of place where bats might rise any second to wheel and dip around our heads.

"The doors could be opened and closed by a single mechanism," the ranger said. "If you stay here, I'll open them and close them again for you."

We stood, shifting our feet, staring around. Up high, facing the cells was a platform all meshed in. A guy pointed up. He was a big manly looking guy with a bald head and a droopy mustache. "That was the gun gallery," he said. "Guards patroled it night and day."

The woman with the crutches was next to me. "Nice place," I said. "How are you doing?"

She twisted her face. "Not so great. I think I might skip what's left of the tour and wait for the rest of you at the dock. There were benches down there, under cover." She was peering at me in the half gloom. "You're kind of lost in that jacket, aren't you? I didn't recognize you." Her hand came up and touched the hood. "Don't pull that around your face or you'll disappear altogether."

My heart gave a lurch. She'd said it! She'd said it exactly! Suppose I didn't give the jacket back? Suppose when we got to Pier 43 I kept the hood up tight around my face, and stayed in the middle of the group? The Outlaws would be looking for a guy in a T-shirt. They'd be sure to miss me.

Then I pictured Maxie's eyes dancing all over the crowd, searching me out. He'd never miss me! Maxie missed nothing. But by the time I got back, the dark clouds might have spread over the city. That's what usually happens when there's rain and fog across the bay. Everyone would be hurrying ...

24

running. I looked at the woman with the crutches, and I wanted to hug her. Maybe I'd get out of this alive after all.

The ranger's voice rolled up the emptiness of Broadway. "I'm opening the doors now." There was a grating of machinery and then the clatter as all the metal doors slid open together.

"Closing," the ranger said.

The barred doors clattered back, shutting with a crash. The noise was deafening. It stayed with us, smashing against our ears. Little by little the echoes died away, leaving the same heavy silence as before. I thought the closing of those doors was the worst sound I'd ever heard in my life.

"Wow!" someone breathed.

We stood, huddled together for comfort.

Once that final crash had told a prisoner he was caged, maybe forever.

The ranger came back. "The doors could be opened and closed singly too. There is a numbered lever that allowed the guard to open one individual cell. But I always find it more effective to do them together, the way it was done, for instance, when they came back from mealtimes."

I looked around the pale, strained faces. It had been effective all right.

"Follow me," the ranger said, and we all scampered behind him. Nobody was anxious to be left behind. Even my friend on her crutches had found new energy. I was trying to think. Was there anything else I could do to disguise myself? Sure! The sunglasses in the pocket. I was feeling better every minute.

"They stopped using Alcatraz as a prison in 1963." The ranger's voice came and went in my brain, through my own flurry of thoughts. "The concrete at the back of the cells had softened with age. The authorities were afraid the prisoners might dig through it and escape. A few did manage to dig their way out. They didn't get very far, of course..."

I thought of the water surrounding the island as the ranger continued. "It was too expensive to upgrade Alcatraz, so it was shut down and the inmates transferred to other federal penitentiaries."

"I'll bet they were all broken up about that," someone said, and everyone laughed. But the laughter sounded pretty hollow.

The ranger stopped to show us railed-off steps that led down into darkness. "The dungeons."

When he turned again we scurried after him, tripping over ourselves to keep up. There was something about this place that made you dread being alone. He stopped around the corner. This bottom row of cells was different. Six of them had solid metal doors.

"The prisoners called these "the hole." There were no lights, no beds. Just an empty box with metal walls and metal floors. For extreme misconduct a prisoner was sent here. Sometimes his clothing was taken away. He slept naked on that metal floor — if he slept."

We craned our necks to see past him.

"No toilet," someone said.

"Just a grating in the floor," the ranger told him. "If anyone would like to go in, to see how it feels in the hole, I'll close the door for a few seconds. I promise you I won't forget and leave you behind. We haven't lost a visitor yet."

About six of us crowded into a cell. The bald guy was with us. The ranger put his body weight against the door and slowly, slowly it began to close. The square of gray, half-light that lay across the metal floor grew narrower. There was a sound like a cork coming out of a bottle, a strange, sucking sound as the last light vanished and the door sealed tight. Darkness swelled around us.

It was total darkness. I'd never imagined a blackness so black. Even at night on the outside it's never really dark. If you squint you can see the outline of a window, or the reflection of a mirror. If you try even harder you can see the shape of your dresser and chair. But here you could squint till your eyes popped out and you'd never see a thing. Being in a coffin twelve feet underground couldn't be any darker. I wished I hadn't thought of a coffin. It suddenly seemed hard to breathe. Panic began to sweep over me. I could hear my heart beating.

There's something about being closed in that freaks you out, even when it's light. And however hard I tried, the thought of my dad kept coming back. Was there a hole where he was? Did he molder away at the end in a place like this? There was no sound anywere. It would just be for a few seconds, the ranger had said. He'd open the door soon. I'd count to twenty and by then I'd be standing outside with the others again, in daylight, with real air to breathe.

"I hope he meant it that he never lost anyone." It was a woman's voice, trying to be casual and missing by a mile.

"Dark, isn't it?" someone else said and giggled. But we were all freaking out.

Open it, open it, open it, I whispered inside my head, and then I heard, or felt, or sensed someone pass me. He was banging on the door right by my head and screaming, "Let me out. Enough's enough. This isn't funny."

I cringed back against the cold steel wall, and then I heard a sob.

"It's okay," another voice said from somewhere on the other side of the cell. "He's going to let us out."

I didn't hear the ranger's footsteps. I guess in this tomb you couldn't see, couldn't breathe and couldn't hear, either. But the door was opening. The shaft of light widened and spread.

We were pushing against each other to get out. The first one free was the big guy with the bald head. His face was gray, and he walked away from the rest of us and stood by himself. I knew he'd been the one hammering on the door.

"It wasn't locked, you know," the ranger said. "You could have pushed it open if you'd put some weight behind it." He looked around. "So, what did you think?"

"I'd rather be skiing," a young guy in a parka said with a sick sort of grin.

"Want to guess how long you were in there?" the ranger asked.

"Five minutes?"

"Four?"

Ranger Rick held up his wrist and showed his watch with the sweeping second hand. "Exactly a minute and a half."

"Naw!"

"How time passes when you're having fun," a woman said. I knew her voice. She'd been one of the few to speak inside. Baldy said nothing. He stood, caressing his mustache, getting his color back. You could tell by looking at him that he was a tough guy, afraid of nothing. Hah! Actually, I liked the bald guy a lot. It's always reassuring to me when somebody else is scareder than I am. Or as scared. I don't come across that situation too often. Gran says I probably do, but I don't recognize it. Like right now. Maybe the others in our cell didn't know it was Baldy who'd cried and hammered on the door. They probably thought it was me. I whistled softly and tried to look tough.

"How would you like to be in there for a week or two?" Ranger Rick asked, his eyes still on our faces. And I tried again not to think of my dad. A week or two? Try a couple of years!

"We'll go in the shower rooms, the dining room and the recreation yard next."

My friend with the crutches leaned against the wall.

"Will it be all right if I make my own way back," she said. "I've had it. It's straight down that road, right?"

The ranger rubbed at his fringe of beard. "Well, ma'am, I don't like to think of you going down alone. Why don't you just wait outside and we'll come back for you."

I could tell the woman didn't want to wait outside these creepy cells by herself even in full daylight, and I didn't blame her. Down below was the ranger station, and maybe a ranger or two walking around, and normal things like rest rooms and drinking fountains. But she didn't have much choice. We all escorted her outside. The rain was more like wet mist now, dripping from trees, hanging in the air. The woman pulled her raincoat around her.

We were just turning away when she called. "Is that another boat coming over?"

I looked across the murkiness of the bay and saw another tour boat on its way to the island, about halfway across.

"That's the three o'clock boat, ma'am," the ranger said. "It's bringing over the last tour. It'll take the group ahead of us back with it."

"If I left now, could I make it back to the city on it?"

"Well..." I could see Ranger Rick didn't want her to go.

"I'm awfully tired," she said. "I should never have come."

"I'll go back with her." I spoke quickly because I'd just thought of something terrific. The Outlaws wouldn't be expecting me on an earlier boat. Who'd rush back into the jaws of death? I'd walk with the crutch lady when she got off, holding her arm like she was my mother or something. In my trusty red-riding hood and black shades, they'd never spot me. "I don't mind. Honest," I said.

And I heard the woman who'd been in the cell with us say to the ranger in a very confidential

A. FRANK SMITH, JR. LIBRARY CENTER
SOUTHWESTERN UNIVERSITY
GEORGETOWN, TEXAS 78626

3 3053 00245 0344

voice, "The kid was really upset back there in the hole. He probably has had enough."

I knew it! They all thought I'd been the phantom pounder. I stole a glance at Baldy who was fully recovered and looking as manly as ever. So? What did I care? It was working out better for me this way.

Ranger Rick rubbed his beard again as if it were Aladdin's lamp and he expected a genie to come and tell him what to do. Then he made his decision.

"All right. You can't miss it. Just follow the road all the way to the bottom. Don't step off the path or go anywhere there's a rope or barricade." Who'd want to?

We set off.

It's not easy hurrying down a switchback path with a lady on crutches! A *wet*, switchback road! We kept urging each other on with reports of where the boat was now, and how much longer it would take us to get to the dock.

At the top of the first rise in the road, we stopped to catch our breath.

The boat was moored. The last tour of the day had started to mill off. There weren't as many getting off as waited to get on. I eyeballed the waiting group. It was the kind of crowd I could get lost in. We hurried on.

"You did great," I told my new friend. "My

name's Danny, and I'll stay with you on the boat and help you off."

But there was one thing I hadn't remembered — how fast that boat emptied. The people streamed from it as if it was the Titanic about to slide under. And the ones getting on were just as speedy.

The three new rangers had the new visitors gathered around the platform already. After all this, after us almost breaking our necks on that dumb winding road, the boat was going to take off and leave us behind. My lady was hobbling as fast as she could.

"Hey! On the boat!" I shouted. "Wait up! We're coming."

She had a good pair of lungs too. "Don't you dare go without us," she yelled.

Everyone turned to look at us ploughing our way down the last lap.

I stopped.

The crutch lady was staring at me, saying, "What's wrong? What's the matter?"

I couldn't have told her what was the matter.

Cowboy, Maxie, Jelly Bean and Priest were standing behind the mob gathered around the rangers.

Maxie's body wriggled and jumped, his head bobbed. He cradled his black box. I could see his crazy, wavery grin. Fat Priest grinned at me too, tapping something unseen against the palm of his hand. I knew what it was. Jelly Bean waved a hand. "Hi, Daddy-Boy," he called. Cowboy smiled.

I felt sick. Why hadn't I thought of this? The Outlaws hadn't waited for me to come to them. They'd come for me.

CHAPTER

4

Afterwards, crouched in my hiding place, I thought of a bunch of things I could have done. I went over them all. I could have run past those guys and jumped on the boat. Of course, they could have turned and jumped on after me, and I'd have ended up in the bay with one of our famous great white sharks munching on my behind. The Outlaws are good at cornering you where there's no one around, and they'd have found someplace, even on a crowded ferry.

I could have headed for the ranger hut. But I knew nothing about that hut. Maybe it was filled with rangers, armed to the gills. Maybe there was no one in there, and the Outlaws could have trapped me. I decided what I did might have been best.

First, of course, I froze totally. I just stood there, my blood pumping in my ears, staring at the four of them. Maxie took a step toward me, but Cowboy put a hand on his arm and said something. Knowing Cowboy, it was probably only a word or two, like "Later" or "Cool it, man."

My friend on her crutches was galloping for the boat. She looked over her shoulder at me. "Come on, Danny."

I opened my mouth but no words came.

She stopped. "What's wrong? Come on. We have to hurry."

"I'm . . ." I swallowed. "I'm going back," I yelled. "Changed my mind," and I spun around and began running back up the switchback road, running and running like a rat for its hole. The cold, wet air gusted across my face. My breath came hard and burning. I stumbled on some loose gravel and risked a look back.

The boat was a few yards from shore, its nose turned toward San Francisco. The group of people on the dock had split into three, the way ours had done. I could see Cowboy and the others, all in one bunch. They were walking with the rest of the tourists, starting up the road, the very road that I was on. Oh, please!

I tried to stay cool and think. But it's hard to

stay cool when a gang's after you, and I suddenly realized that I was on an island — a small one — with no way off till that boat came back. It's weird, the feeling I got. Like a trapped animal. Like a prisoner. Why hadn't they run after me as soon as they'd seen me? Because it was more fun for them this way. Cowboy had put his hand on Maxie's arm and whispered something. Probably that there was no hurry. That they should let me sweat.

Below me the group trailed up the path, following their leader in his Smokey Bear hat. I had no trouble picking out my four. Cowboy's brown and red checked shirt, his hat that was almost as wide as the ranger's. Jelly Bean's dark green football jersey with the big numbers on it. I could even read the 22 from here. Maxie in a red, long sleeved T-shirt and Priest in the black jeans and black shirt he always wore, little fat creep that he was. Nobody had bothered to lend *them* jackets on the boat. They were the kind of guys people instinctively stayed away from.

Why was I standing here? Because I didn't know what else to do, that was why. My eyes searched the scrubby road that curved bleak and dismally upward. On one side was the drop to the ocean, fringed with scraggly, wind-bruised bushes. On the other was untended grass and then the rock, running up to where the prison sat. I had to go on because I couldn't go back. Maybe I could join up again with my tour. I'd stick close by Ranger Rick. Heck, I'd hold his hand, if necessary. But that wouldn't stop the Outlaws. If they got within striking distance they'd strike, even if the whole of the San Francisco riot squad was surrounding me.

My eyes were jumping around like Maxie's, searching, searching. To my right now, across a rope and a stretch of weeds and long grass was the big water tower. Two ladders led up its sides to the reservoir on top. I'd be like a fly on a wall going up one of those ladders. They'd all see me. Maybe Jelly Bean would throw his knife. Jelly Bean could do just about anything with that big old heavy knife. I'd seen him plenty of times in the park, flinging it at trees, the blade sticking in the bark, the bone handle quivering like an arrow. I scrunched up my shoulders.

And then I saw it. The hole in the ground! The morgue!

In two seconds I was over the rope that blocked it from the road and I was inside. It was a square, concrete room, almost dark, the ground littered with windblown leaves and small branches. There was a rusted sink in the corner, a broken wall cabinet and a stone slab table. I wished the door was still there so I could close it behind me.

I crouched against the wall to the right of the door space, out of sight of anyone who would pass, squinching my eyes tight closed, listening. There was nothing to hear but the small puffs of wind rattling the leaves across the floor and something else, a sliding something. I popped my eyeballs open. An old Fritos bag blew this way and that, against the slab table. A paper cup rolled drunkenly by the wall.

And now I heard the feet trudging up the path, the muted sound of voices. My right knee was cramping. I pounded it with my fist.

The feet had stopped.

"This was the morgue," the ranger said. "The prisoners could see inside it on the way up to their cells for the first time."

It was the same patter we'd had. They probably all went to ranger school. I held my leg to keep it from jerking.

A kid's voice piped up, "Can we go inside?"

My heart leaped into my mouth. I swallowed it down and felt it slither back into place.

"No. You can't go in. See that rope? That means it's off limits."

"Why?"

The little guy was going to argue, maybe even whine a bit, and the ranger would give in and let him take a peek inside, and he'd see me and he'd yell, "Hey! There's a guy here!" And the Outlaws would be across that rope in one screaming leap. Who said the morgue wasn't in use anymore? They'd lay me out like a turkey on that cold stone slab.

"Why can't you go in?" The ranger had raised his voice. "I've just told you why not. It's off limits. And I would like to caution all of you that anywhere that is roped off is roped off for a reason. Probably because the area is dangerous. These are old, unused buildings. The flooring is unsafe. Walls and ceilings fall. Please, for your own safety, observe our rules and don't make any attempt to go where you're not supposed to go."

I held my breath.

The ranger went on with his spiel about how for some prisoners, death was the only way out of Alcatraz. The first time I'd heard those words, they'd run through my head and left little trace. Now I was really hearing them. Now they seemed spoken just for me.

"We'll go on up the road now," the ranger said. "I apologize for our weather. I'm sure some of you aren't too comfortable but soon we'll be inside, under shelter."

The voices and feet were trailing away. And then I heard Maxie's giggle. Close.

"Where are you headin' for Jelly Bean?" Maxie asked. "You'll be in a morgue soon enough, man."

My heart came back to my throat because a long, string-bean, jelly-bean figure was in the doorway.

I couldn't see him, but I could sense him. I could smell him the way a dog smells danger. He was there. He didn't come all the way in, standing about a foot back, looking. If he came forward and turned his head, he'd spot me. I sensed him leave.

"Don't go wandering off, Bean," Cowboy said. "Stay together." The voices dwindled away.

I stood up, shaking. My right leg was so cramped that it doubled beneath me and I grabbed for the wall. The plaster crumbled like chalk under my hand.

There had to be a way out of this.

I peered along the path. They had all disappeared around the upper bend. Okay. I was behind them now. They didn't know where I was, but I knew where they were. That had to be an advantage.

My new instinct was to run back down the path. When the boat came again I'd be close to it. That would be the boat for *my* tour, Ranger Rick's tour. But I knew instantly and certainly that the Outlaws would come down and check that boat. They'd be thinking ahead of me. Stuff like this was easy for them. I tried to work it out. There'd be two more boats — mine and theirs. They'd be watching both of them. Whichever one I got on, they'd find me.

The rain had stopped and I stood in the cold, damp air. I was shivering and however hard I tried to think, nothing came.

My friend, Curt, had told me just yesterday what

he would do if he were me. "Look," he'd said. "You can't keep away from them forever. They're going to get you, Danny. You might as well face it. Why don't you just let them catch you and get it over with? Then you'll be free."

I'd stared at him. "Are you crazy? Look at what they did to Alan Foster. " It made me shiver just to think about it. The Outlaws had locked him in a locker after school, and if the cleaning man hadn't heard him shouting and let him out, he could have suffocated. "And that was just because Alan wouldn't let Maxie copy his term paper," I added.

"Alan Foster should have had more sense," Curt said. "He ought to know you don't say no to the Outlaws. Listen, Danny, before they come at you, remind them that you didn't know that that guy was Priest's brother. And remind them that you wouldn't testify against him, even when the cops wanted you to."

"Well, even *I* had more sense than to do that."

"Tell them quick that you'll pay for the kid's new glasses."

"I *told* them that already. It made no difference. They don't think the way other people think, Curt."

Curt shook his head. "That's what I'd do anyway. Give yourself up and get it over with."

But that would take a lot of guts. It would be like walking into the dentist's when you don't have a toothache and saying, "I think I might get a toothache ten years from now in this molar over here, so why don't you just do a root canal on it while I wait. I've got nothing better to do today, anyway." One thing for sure. Alcatraz Island was no place to hand myself over. Offhand, I couldn't think of any place that was.

I stood, getting my mind together, and I decided that the best and smartest thing to do right now was to go down and check out that ranger station. So what if I sounded paranoid? That's one advantage of being small. With any luck the rangers would think I was a little kid, twelve or so. I could snivel like a kid if I had to. I'd beg them to take care of me. For an instant I thought about Biddy. She might be there, and I'd have to snivel in front of her. But I didn't care. I thought, too, about how much worse it would be for me later, because I'd snitched. The heck with that. I needed to survive now.

I ran a zigzag course down the hill in case any of the Outlaws caught sight of me. Mean little waves whipped against the jetty. A sailboat, big as a clipper ship, ploughed across the bay. I stopped and waved and called. If only it would put about and come rescue me! I was like one of those silly dudes in movies who's always waving at plumes of smoke on the horizon. But, when you're desperate you'll try anything. The clipper ship moved like a ghost into the gloom, only its mastlight showing it existed.

I lumbered across the dock in front of the restrooms. Everywhere I looked was deserted. I could have been alone on the island, me and a seagull hunched on a piling.

I pushed at the door of the ranger hut. Locked. I pounded and shouted, "Is anyone here?" But no one came. I peered through the window. Empty.

There were four big wooden tables with benches. A hat lay on one. A clipboard, too. A smaller table was just under the window below me. Papers were scattered on it. There was a looseleaf notebook.

Around the back were more windows and another room, empty too. I saw a bunk with a sleeping bag on it. Metal lockers lined the walls, some with the keys still dangling in the locks. Hooks held green ranger jackets and ponchos.

Where was everyone? I remembered the restrooms and I sprinted across.

"Hello!" I yelled through the open door.

The only sound was a faucet dripping and the whistle of the wind gusting across the bay.

No place here to hide either. There's something extra creepy about an empty rest room. I found myself jerking looks over my shoulder. The Outlaws could have moseyed back down here looking for me. They could have split up. I wondered if I could handle two of them, desperate as I was, and I tried to pick the two I'd want. But I didn't want any of them. I backed up. Once I read that thieves hardly ever go in the bathroom when they rob a house. They figure a bathroom can be a trap with its little windows and its solid walls. I got out of this one fast and stood, uncertain.

The first lights were flickering across the bay. I could see the tiny hanging bulbs outlining the bridges. Yellow squares checkerboarded the high-rises. Offices. People getting ready to go home. They'd come down and get in their cars or buses, or head for the nearest cable car stop or Bart station. The city looked close enough to swim to. I had such an ache I couldn't stand it.

Gran would be puttering around now, fixing supper. She'd have the Mary Tyler Moore show on. The programs were all on their umpteenth reruns, but Gran never missed them. I had a lump in my throat. Man, who would have thought I'd be crying over Mary and Lou and dopey old Ted? Mom would be home soon. It would be a while though before they'd begin worrying about me.

At that minute, I felt like the last man on earth. I swear, if the Outlaws had come down I'd have been almost glad to see them. Almost.

The seagull rose, and flew screeching over my head. I had to go. Now. Back to my hole. Back to safety. There was a piece of jagged concrete by the side of the path and I hefted it, feeling its good sharp edges. Then I ran, stumbling up the hill.

In the morgue I sat, scrunched against the wall, the hunk of rock between my feet. Already I knew what I was going to do. Somewhere, in the time I'd stood looking across the bay it had come to me. I'd stay on Alcatraz overnight. The Outlaws would go, on this boat or the next one. Somehow they'd think they'd missed me. In the morning I'd join up with the first tour group to leave the island. The rangers would never notice an extra person in the crowd and I'd get home and be safe.

I didn't want to stay on this dark, ghost island. I was scared stupid. But I didn't have any choice.

CHAPTER

5

I heard Ranger Rick's tour come down the hill and I let it pass. I heard the toot as the boat came in and the toot as it went out.

Still I sat.

It wasn't quite dark yet, but on a day like this the dark would come early, swallowing up the island, dragging it down into the sea. Maybe that's what happened to it at night. Anything was possible in a place like this. I could see cold-eyed sharks, swimming along Broadway, their split tails waving back and forth among seaweed that swayed from the bars of cells. An octopus, curling itself in the corner of the black hole. A moray eel, its great jaws snapping out from that underground dungeon, its head waving and bobbing on the end of its thick scaly neck. A ghost island. And tonight I'd go down with it.

I shivered and tried not to bawl. No kidding, I was so scared and cold and lonely I felt about six years old.

I thought about my father and how it might have been if I'd ever known him. Would I have been different? Maybe I would have been braver. Maybe I'd have fought the Outlaws, single-handed, instead of hiding from them.

I heard the last tour come down, and I heard the last boat, and I waited, imagining the Outlaws checking everyone going on, getting mad at each other and yelping because somehow they'd missed me. A few minutes later I heard the forlorn toot as the boat pulled away from shore. I dragged myself up and went outside. Every muscle in my body was cramped.

The boat was almost out of sight. It went in a dark churn of foam, spreading white at its stern. There was warmth in the glow of the lighted cabin. Inside there'd be coffee smells, spilt popcorn crunching underfoot, the buzz of voices. The visitors were going home and I was here. I'd let the boat go without me, and I was glad, because in that nice cozy cabin or on that half lighted deck the Outlaws would be prowling, buzzing like hornets, still looking for me.

It was dark where I stood in front of the open mouth of the morgue. All at once I was aware of the little noises around me. Somewhere, far away, there was a clanking, like a chain rattling. The wind strummed softly through the slats that supported the water tower. The waves hissed and whispered against the dock. From somewhere in the bay a buoy clanged.

Below me, the cement area by the dock lay in pale pools of lamplight surrounded by shadows. The warning beam from the lighthouse slithered across the black water. Above me the old prison lay dead, filled with its own memories.

When something brushed against my leg I gave a yelp.

Two yellow eyes shone up at me and I felt the slinky pressure of the cat against my wet jeans.

"You scared the spit out of me," I said out loud. "Where did you come from?" I bent to stroke the cat. Its fur was soft and wet and a bunch of hairs came off on my hand. I wiped them away on my jeans. The cat's purring was the best thing I'd heard all day. "I nearly fainted, you know that, cat?" I said. "Come on," and I began hurrying down the hill.

And then I saw a movement at the side of the

restroom. A man came from behind it — a ranger, wearing a ranger hat and a slick black poncho, and swinging something in his hand. Relief was a great tide of warmth in my stomach. There was someone here. I'd been telling myself that there had to be, but underneath I hadn't been sure.

I lifted my arm to wave and began to call. But the shout died in my throat. Another ranger was coming from behind the rest rooms, a little fat one in a green ranger jacket, and now there was a third and a fourth, in ranger jackets too, the last one carrying something big and square. A radio! I knew instantly who they were. The Outlaws. The tide of warmth in my stomach ebbed away and left some strange, wiggling things crawling inside me. How could I have thought I could outsmart them? They had stayed too.

The cat miaowed and I bent and pushed it away. "Go! Scat!" I couldn't afford cat noises or any kind of noises. I couldn't afford to breathe.

Why hadn't I figured on this? I should have. From somewhere I remembered me and Bobby Blue talking about his pigeons.

"The Outlaws had to go right by my bedroom window and past my parents' windows to get to the roof. That door up there squeals like a son of a gun, and I know my birds. They're noisy. My Dad's a real light sleeper. Nobody heard a thing. What a nerve those guys have!"

"They probably enjoyed it," I'd told him. "If it's not risky its not worth it, you know? And when it's scary and they win, they feel bigger than ever. It's like a game."

I'd been such a wise guy when it was Bobby Blue's pigeons. But now it was me. I was their game. Somehow they'd slipped away from the rangers who'd been herding the people onto the boat. Somehow they'd gotten into the ranger hut and taken the jackets and who knew what else. Probably broke one of the windows at the back. The Outlaws wouldn't care. Now they were warm and comfortable. Now they were ready.

They kept to the shadows by the rest rooms, running quickly and quietly across the open lighted space to the darkness of the road.

My knees had turned to squish.

"Miaow," the cat said, right beside me and I spun around and started running fast up the hill. I had to hide. Not in the morgue, though. Now that they were searching, they'd look everywhere. And that's the kind of place those freaks would think of right away. Of course, it would be black in there, and I didn't think they had a light. But they'd feel their way around and find me, cowering with the Fritos bag in the darkest corner. No way! Talk about a rat in a trap.

I saw the white gleam of the water tower then, and I knew it was the perfect place. I'd climb it, higher and higher. From up there, I'd be able to see where they were. And something else. I'd be able to fend them off. I had a picture of myself crouched on that platform that ran around the tank, waiting for them to come up the ladders. It would be a fort, and I could hold it forever. If only I had a cannon up there! If only I had my nice, sharp hunk of concrete! But I'd left it in the morgue and I wasn't going back for it. I wasn't taking that kind of chance.

I hunched along the path feeling with my hands for a rock, for anything. But all I found was gravelly dirt, the biggest pieces no heavier than a dime. I shoveled some of it into the pockets of my jacket and then I wriggled under the warning rope and ploughed through the long grass to the tower.

The ladders were metal, attached to the crisscross scaffolding that supported the big tank on top. And I couldn't reach them — the first rungs started way above my head. I jumped, but I still couldn't reach them. Oh, no! Why wasn't I bigger? A few more inches would have done it. I tried climbing the wooden slats below, but I had no handhold and I slid back down.

They were coming. Any minute now I'd hear the shuffle of their feet on the path. They'd see me here, behind this shrimpy wooden scaffolding. And there was nowhere to run.

I walked backwards as far as I could without dropping off the edge of the island, and then I ran for the ladder. I ran the way a guy runs coming up for the broad jump, or with a pole in his hand to vault over the bar. The way a guy runs when he's about to be caught.

My teeth were clenched; I had to reach that ladder. My eyes were fixed on its glimmer and I jumped, feeling my muscles pop. My feet skidded on the long wet grass, but I had enough thrust for the leap. One hand was around the bottom rung, slithering, slipping, but I got the other hand on and held. I reached for the rung above, my tennies flat against the wooden slats, and then I had that rung too. My feet scrambled, walking me up till they were on the bottom rung and I was climbing. I didn't look down. And I prayed they wouldn't look up.

I didn't stop till the big, gray-white tank hid me from the path below. For now I would go no higher. They might see me against the sky as I climbed onto the platform.

For the first time I looked down. The Outlaws were on the road. They seemed small from here, like stunted midgets. The cat had attached itself behind them. They passed the water tower area and as I watched, one of them stepped over the rope that stretched in front of the morgue. I'd been right. They weren't going to miss any hiding place. A light beam sliced across the darkness . . . a wide, white, bright beam, bigger than a flashlight. It was a lantern, the powerful kind electricians use. Somewhere they'd found that too. Behind it, I saw the wide shadowy brim of Cowboy's hat and the dark, shortened tent of his poncho. Cowboy stood in the doorway. The other three went inside.

I heard a horse laugh that I recognized as Jelly Bean's, and then they were all outside again. If I'd been hiding there, they'd have had me for sure. I pressed myself as tightly as I could against the big metal reservoir. The truth was, if I could see them they could see me, too, if they looked up this far. Please don't let them look up, I prayed.

I don't know how long I stood there. A big, silent tanker, lit from bow to stern, was moving across the bay. I waited till it glided all the way under the bridge. Then I waited till a little fishing boat with a green light on the side closest to me chugged its way past Angel Island. Ten minutes I waited. Maybe more.

A small plane flew right above me, its engines whirring like a lawn mower. I wanted to wave, but the wind and the height made me too scared. If only the crew would see me and radio in. "We saw something over on Alcatraz. Somebody's hiding there. He's halfway up the water tower. Better send a chopper over and check it out."

No chance. I'd be only a black dot in the darkness from up there.

My hands were numb now. Each gust of wind tried to pluck me from my perch and probably would have if I hadn't been weighed down by a half a ton of gravel in each pocket. But I couldn't hold on much longer.

I climbed up, got my leg over the railing, and was on the platform that ran around the tank. The big reservoir loomed scaly above me. There were square, faded letters on its side, ghost letters from a time past, like everything else on Alcatraz. I padded around the tank, sheltered from the wind on one side, getting the whack of it on the other. Looking down, I could see the whole island, from the big, square administration building to the crumble of the old parade grounds. I could even look inside the warden's house, roofless now, a box without a lid. And I could see the Outlaws . . . or at least two of them. No, three.

They were crossing what I guess had once been the recreation yard. There were broken rows of concrete bleachers and an empty cement area, wired and walled off. As I watched, two of them checked behind the solid sides of the concrete seats. I took a shaky breath. They weren't going to lose me this time. They knew I was here somewhere, and if I was here they would find me. They'd search all through the empty hours of the night. How long would it be before one of them thought of this water tower?

I took the handfuls of gravel from one pocket and piled them at the top of the first ladder. Then I ran around and put the other pile at the top of the second ladder. The wind instantly took the small stones and whisked them away. I ran back to the first ladder. There was no way I could guard both of them at once; they were too far apart. Suppose I did try to fend off two of the Outlaws as they came up one ladder? The other two would be on me from the other side.

What I needed was to forget the heroics and find some way to get help.

I ran around the tower again, butting against the wind, trying to see where the Outlaws were now. I'd lost them. But I knew they were somewhere up by the recreation yard, far from me. There'd be time enough for me to get to the ranger station. Time enough to pray that a ranger would be there.

I went down the ladder almost as fast as I'd come up, glad of the rusted places on the wet metal that gave my fingers a better grip. I didn't look down until I was almost on the ground, and I only looked then because I heard a noise. That noise froze me. It was a cough. And it was right below me.

I hung there, a few feet above the last rung, with nowhere to hide.

A dark figure crouched on the ground. There was a flicker that was blown out in the wind, then another. A match. It went out again almost immediately and then I heard a laugh and a voice called:

"You up there Daddy-Boy? You left a liddle mark here, fellow. Little skid mark. Little-biddie foodprits

56

going up the wood toward that ladder. Daddy-Boy?"

Jelly Bean!

He jumped and caught the bottom rung.

"There you are Daddy-Boy. I'b cubbing to get you."

Even as the words were plucked from him and flown away on the wind he was swarming toward me, fast as a spider in a web. And I just stood there like a bug-eyed fly, waiting.

CHAPTER

6

At first I was paralyzed with fear, but then I got such a spurt of panic that I moved faster than I ever thought I could. I began thrashing up the ladder, but I could hear Jelly Bean close behind me, so close that I knew his reaching hands were only a couple of rungs below me.

As I tried to get away, terror made my feet move too quickly and I stumbled, losing the pattern of the climb, slowing myself down. My breath tore at my throat. There was sweat in my eyes, and the ladder above me went out of focus. The rungs melted into each other, the metal tilted at a crazy angle. I blinked and stopped. A hand closed on my right ankle.

I struggled, clinging to the bars, hooking my left foot around the outside rail.

Jelly Bean yanked. My arms were jarred so badly that they almost came from their sockets.

"Let go!" I wound my arms frantically around the bars.

Jelly Bean jerked again.

I unhooked my free leg from the side rail and kicked back at his hand. He swore loudly, the words softened by the wind. Then my ankle was free.

I glanced frantically down between my legs and saw his arm reaching up again, and I don't know exactly what happened in the next second or how it happened. I think Jelly Bean came up another rung just as I kicked again. He fell like a clown doing a funny backward dive into a pool.

I clung to the ladder and turned my face against its cold, wet rungs. My stomach was heaving. Over and over I kept saying, "Oh please. Oh please. I didn't mean to do it!" I couldn't get myself to move either up or down. It was so easy to fall, to drop back into that space, to crash to the ground below. And where were the rest of the Outlaws? Were they all down there, bending over Jelly Bean, starting to climb up after me and get me for getting him? They wouldn't listen if I said I hadn't meant to do it. I hadn't meant to turn Priest's brother over to the cops either. I never meant to do anything.

I forced my head to turn. I forced myself to look down. Jelly Bean lay, spread out on his back in a nest of grass and weeds. I could see the pale blob of his face. He looked as if he could get up any second and start after me again.

The thought lubricated my locked arms and legs and I began climbing. Wait. It would be better to go down and try to get around him. Even if he tried to catch me, he'd be slower now after the fall. I'd get away. If the rest of them weren't waiting to ambush me as soon as I set foot on the ground.

Where were they? Although it was dark, there was a glow from the sky. The lighthouse beam left the night untouched here, but as it turned I could see nothing in any direction except the wind torn grass and wind bent trees. Maybe Jelly Bean had wandered off alone again, the way he'd done when he went in the morgue. If the other Outlaws were nearby they would surely have gone over to him when he fell.

I came down all the way, slowly, my eyes flickering to the path and the cliff drop and the far stretch of grass. I let myself fall as I dropped from the last step and I lay very still, listening. There was nothing to hear but the sighing of the wind in the tall weeds and its whistle through the slats. I thought I could hear the soft fall of light rain touching the metal above me and there was the sound of the sea, its murmur like blood in the arteries of the island.

Only a small space separated me now from Jelly Bean, and my insides began to heave again. I'd keep to my plan and run away. First, though, I'd go over there and check him out. I didn't want to, but I knew I had to.

I edged through the grass at a crouch.

Jelly Bean lay limp and relaxed, comfortable looking in his springy bed. His eyes were closed and his mouth open. I bent over him. He hadn't been up that far on the ladder, not really. Maybe ten feet at most. I wished I had a light and then I remembered his matches. They'd be in his pocket. My hands didn't want to go near his pockets or him, but I made them.

I sheltered the match's small flame in my hand and held it by Jelly Bean's head. All the time I was looking over my shoulder, keeping an eye out for the rest of the Outlaws. It was creepy the way the light flickered across Jelly Bean's face, turning his nose into a beak that threw its hooked shadow onto his chin. I didn't see any blood. I made myself light another match, and it was then that I noticed his leg. It was bent under him. I don't know much about stuff like that, but even I could tell the leg was broken and he was unconscious. The flame blew out and I was glad. I didn't want to look at Jelly Bean anymore. What I wanted to do was get away before his friends found me.

There had to be somebody in that ranger station. There had to be.

I dropped the matches in my pocket, turned and ran across the grass under the tower. And it was then that I saw the white beam of a flashlight bobbing toward me down the path.

I hit the grass, belly down. Whoever was coming was not moving quietly. He was whistling! Whistling an old Elton John song that I'd heard a million times.

I raised my head about a tenth of an inch and peered through the darkness that lay behind the bobbing ball of light.

It was someone in dark pants and jacket. A ranger, or someone pretending to be a ranger. I looked back at where Jelly Bean lay and could see nothing. He was sunken, deep in his grassy nest.

The figure had passed before I recognized it. The ranger wore no hat and the forward glow of light made a red halo around the great mass of hair. It was Biddy!

"Biddy!" I was whispering in case the Outlaws could hear . . . in case I would waken Jelly Bean.

She didn't hear me either. The light bounced on.

"Biddy!" I ran frantically after her.

The flashlight wavered. The figure turned and the beam moved till it reached my face.

"It's me. Remember? The boy on the boat. You got me this jacket?" I couldn't believe my voice. It didn't sound like me. Maybe I'd turned into somebody else?

She was walking back to meet me. "What on earth are you doing here? Everybody's gone. Why didn't you leave on the boat?" She stopped in front of me.

I didn't move. "Look," I said in my new not-me voice. "We've got to get the cops out here. And an ambulance. There's somebody hurt bad. And ..." I suddenly realized we were standing there, talking, not even keeping our voices down, and this place was crawling with danger. "We've got to go," I whispered grabbing her arm. "There's a gang here. They came out after me and ..."

"Wait. Wait just a second." I could sense her disbelief. She pulled her arm away. "Let's take this one thing at a time. First off, we'll go down to the ranger hut. Maybelline should be there now, and you can tell us all about it. Did ..."

She stopped.

Neither of us had heard the Outlaws come up behind us. They can move as quietly as lizards when they want to. The way they did when they crept up on Bobby Blue's pigeons. I heard Maxie's giggle, and I knew we were lost.

The big beacon in Cowboy's hand was a searchlight that fastened itself on Biddy's face. It paled the beam she shone on them.

"What? . . ." Biddy faltered. "Who are you? Are you rangers?" Her voice trailed off, and I could see she couldn't figure what was going on. They looked like rangers, from the waist up, anyway. The cat was cradled in Cowboy's arms. Its eyes gleamed green in the light.

"What have we here?" Cowboy asked and Maxie grinned and said, "I dunno. But whatever it is, I like it."

Biddy's hand went to somewhere at her waist, under the jacket. It was Maxie who lobbed the radio he carried into Priest's hands and jumped her, pinning her arms. Her flashlight fell and began rolling down the path, stopping with its beam trapped in a tangle of weeds. Maxie pulled Biddy's wrist from under the jacket and in the spotlight's glare I saw a small, pocket-sized transistor. A walkie-talkie, I guess. He pried it from her fingers and gave it to Cowboy.

Cowboy didn't even look down. His arm arched, and he threw the little transistor high and far in the direction of the sea. The cat, squeezed as Cowboy stretched, let out a screech. Cowboy dropped it, and it sprang off into the shadows.

"Aw, Cowboy," Priest said. "We could have had

fun with that." I didn't know if he meant the cat or the walkie-talkie.

"Let me go," Biddy said loudly, and I suddenly realized that Maxie was still holding her with her arm twisted behind her and that nobody was paying any attention to me.

I wheeled around, ducked and began pounding down the hill.

I hadn't taken more than a dozen steps when Cowboy had me. He lifted me, my back to his belly, my feet not touching the ground. I kicked at his shins with my heels and he dumped me on the path. As I scrambled up, something pricked behind my right ear and I rolled my eyes around and saw Priest's fat, creepy face. I swear to heaven he was licking his ugly lips.

"Be good, Danny-Boy," he said, and he pricked me again with the point of the ice pick. I knew I was going to be very good.

"Let her go," Cowboy said, and Maxie took his hands off Biddy. He walked over and picked up the flashlight.

"Look," Biddy said. "I'm a national park ranger. You're trespassing on national park property. I don't know what's going on here, but I'm ordering all of you to come down, now, to the ranger station and explain what you're doing here."

Cowboy sounded amused. "You're ordering?" He

turned and began walking up the path. "Bring Danny Boy," he said over his shoulder. "And bring Little Miss Ranger too."

"What about Bean?" Maxie asked.

"Leave him," Cowboy said. "He's prowling. He'll find us."

"If he could see what we've got, he'd come fast enough." Maxie giggled his scummy giggle.

If they only knew! I had a quick terrible picture of Jelly Bean, lying there with the wind blowing across his closed eyes, lifting and moving his thin, pale hair. I saw the twisted leg. But how could I tell the other Outlaws what I'd done? They'd kill me. My heart thudded. If Jelly Bean didn't get help, he mightn't hack it, and what would that make me? I licked my lips.

"Cowboy?" I began.

The ice pick jabbed behind my ear. "Shut up, turkey. Who asked you to talk?"

"But . . ." The prick was a bee sting. If Priest put his strength behind it, it would be a hole in my head. I shut up.

It was a relief to have tried and failed. "See," I said to whoever was listening to my soundless talk, "I tried. Whatever happens to Jelly Bean now isn't my fault."

Maxie pushed Biddy ahead of him so that she was behind Cowboy. I was behind him with Priest right on my heels.

"Gimme my box," Maxie ordered, and Priest passed over the big stereo radio. Punk music blasted, bouncing off the rocks, setting a group of gulls to screaming and wheeling white against the black sky.

"Shut that off," Cowboy said. "You want the watchman to hear?"

The music slammed into silence. Cowboy had turned off the lantern too, and the darkness was darker than ever as we walked through it.

"You're not going to get away with this," Biddy said. "I can't just disappear. I'm expected down there in the ranger station, and when I don't come they'll start looking for me."

"Don't give us that 'they' stuff," Cowboy said. "There's just one, honey baby. One night watchman."

Maxie giggled. "One dumb old guy. Think we're going to worry about him?" In front of me his head was never still, moving around on his neck like a bobbing doll in a car window. I knew his eyes would be crawling all over Biddy's back. His mind would be crawling all over her too. As I watched, he lifted his hand and touched her hair.

"Stop it," Biddy said.

Priest spoke behind me, his voice raised so Biddy could hear over the wind. "You rangers are pretty stupid, you know it? You know how we found out there's only one watchman? We asked."

Maxie giggled again. That giggle could drive you

to murder. He began to speak in a high-pitched whine. "Do all the rangers leave the island at night Mr. Ranger, sir? They do? But surely someone must stay here? A night watchman? Oh, I see, sir. I expect he's armed? No? Well, of course he doesn't need to be, does he? I don't suppose there's anything anybody would want to steal on a place like this."

Priest jabbed at my back. I couldn't feel the point of the pick through my thick jacket, but I knew it wasn't his finger. "Careless talk costs lives," he said. "I heard that once in an old movie."

"Hey," Maxie said. "I saw that flick too. It was all about the war. Clark Gable and a blond broad."

"Yeah. He was a big shot doctor and she was a nurse."

The drizzle of mist lay on me, cold as death. One night watchman. No gun. If he did come near us the Outlaws could take him, no problem. The only hope now was Maybelline, whoever she was. Maybelline of the big 5–0. She was down in the ranger station too, and the Outlaws didn't know about her.

Cowboy stopped so suddenly that Biddy bumped into him. "What I'm wondering," he said, "is why *you're* here?"

Biddy didn't answer for a minute, and then she said coldly, "Just lucky, I guess."

I sensed Cowboy's smile. Maxie's giggle was as close as he'd ever come to a laugh. He picked up an end of her red hair again and twined it around his finger. "I like her," he said. Biddy's elbow got him low in his stomach — real low. "I said, keep your hands off me, you weirdo!"

Maxie doubled over. "Ohhh . . !" he gasped.

Biddy spoke to Cowboy. "There are a dozen of us here. We stayed because it's Maybelline's birthday. We're having a party for her. You can't handle all of us. Why don't you . . ."

Biddy didn't answer. Cowboy stood looking down at her, and then he said quietly. "I don't think so, honey baby. I think you're lying. I think there's only you. You and us."

"And Danny-Boy," Priest said. "Don't forget Danny-Boy. He has to learn you don't mess with the Outlaws." He was poking me again, hard. "And you don't mess with their brothers." Poke, poke. "Or their mothers." Poke, poke. "Or their dogs." Poke, poke. "Or their friends." Poke, poke. We were walking again now, walking through the falling wetness and the scudding wind toward the old, walled prison.

CHAPTER

7

We went single-file through the big door to the main cell block, past the control room and the small, bare space where visitors once talked through a hole in the wall to husbands, or fathers, or brothers. Somehow I knew we were heading for the place the prisoners called Broadway — the big echoing area between cell blocks. It was the empty heart of this dead prison. Whatever was going to happen would happen there.

As soon as we were under cover, Cowboy switched on the lantern. We paraded up the middle aisle of Broadway, with its rows of cells on either side, and our thin, slanting shadows marched beside us. The beam shone along the endless corridor. There was no sound in here but the shuffle of our feet in the silence. My nose was filled with the damp mustiness of decay. We were like a chain gang, I thought. Chained together, the metal balls dragging behind us.

About halfway along, Cowboy stopped. There was a small wooden platform, about a foot high, in front of one of the cells. The top was no bigger than a coffee table. Ranger Rick had stood on it while he talked to us about the prison and what it had been like for the prisoners here. On the platform he could be seen and heard by everybody. I'd stood at the back of the group, thinking I'd made it away from the Outlaws, feeling pleased with myself. That seemed like a very long time ago.

Cowboy put the lantern on the wooden step but left it switched on. Maxie set his radio and Biddy's flashlight beside it.

"What do we do now, Cowboy?" Priest darted a sideways glance at me, and I swear, for the first time, for the very first time, I wondered what exactly they were going to do with me. Everything had happened so quickly! I'd been struggling to stay away from them, because I knew that whatever they did when they found me would be bad. I'd have to pay. Till now, though, I'd never stopped to think about how I would pay.

Sweat began trickling from hidden pores. Like a collage I saw Jerry Cordelli with the ice pick quivering in his foot; Alan Foster, lugging his big piles of books to and from school because he wouldn't ever go back near his locker. Then I saw one of Bobby Blue's pigeons, its feathers all clotted with blood. I didn't think the Outlaws had ever killed anything except the pigeons. If they had, nobody had told about it, either. Suddenly I needed desperately to go to the bathroom.

Maxie was rattling the bars of one of the cells. "Hey! How do these things open?" Nobody answered.

"Well?" Cowboy stared at Biddy and she stared right back. I realized that the Outlaws hadn't had the complete tour. They hadn't seen the ranger walk to the end of the row and pull the levers. They'd left their group part way along and joined the other one, looking for me. Maybe that could help Biddy and me in some way. Right now I couldn't see how.

Maxie was searching with his hands above the door, looking for a bar or a hidden latch. When Cowboy reached out and cuffed Biddy on the side of her head, she gave a sharp little yelp and rubbed at her ear.

I took a quick step forward and stopped when Priest said in a smiling whisper, "Go ahead. Do something stupid. Be brave, Danny-Boy."

"It's okay," Biddy said quickly. "It didn't hurt. It just surprised me."

"Don't be surprised," Cowboy said and smiled. I'd never noticed what big teeth he had, big and square with gaps between them. I guess I'd never seen him smile before. "Now, one more time. How do the doors open?"

"Down there. They all open together." Biddy's hand still rubbed at her head.

"Show Maxie," Cowboy said and Maxie padded toward us, playing with the switchblade, his eyes twitching from her to me, up the aisle that was Broadway, back to Biddy again. "Show Maxie," he said.

Biddy walked ahead of him and we stood, waiting. I wondered if Cowboy had a knife. I'd heard rumors that he kept one of those old fashioned straight razors in his pocket, but nobody had ever seen it. Suddenly I thought of something. Jelly Bean's big buck knife, the one he kept in a sheath on his belt! I could have taken it. I'd have had it now, hidden under my jacket. I might even have been able to jump the others and save Biddy and me from this nightmare. But even as I thought about the knife I shivered. To sink the blade into soft flesh — I wasn't sure I could have done it.

There was a clanging of metal and then the crash as all the cell doors behind Cowboy ground open.

Maxie's voice echoed down Broadway. "Hey! How do you like that? You want them closed again?"

"Not yet," Cowboy said. "Bring the girl back."

I thought about the watchman. Where was he? And the mysterious Maybelline? Couldn't they hear all this clanging and banging? Only, I guess, if they were nearby. We were high up on the island, behind thick walls. I thought of them sitting snug down in the hut, drinking coffee, talking maybe about how some rotten tourists had come over and ripped off a bunch of ranger jackets and stuff.

What did a watchman find to do on Alcatraz anyway? Did he snoop around to see if everything was all right? Or did he just stay by the dock to turn away any illegal boats that might come in to explore? Why would he bother checking out the prison? As Maxie had said, what was there to rip off in a place like this?

Cowboy nodded toward one of the cells. "Put Danny-Boy there. Her in the one next to him."

Priest pushed me into the cage. Next door, I heard Maxie say: "Easy, baby. Easy." And I knew Biddy wasn't letting herself be shoved around.

I peered up at Priest who was standing in my cell door. The wedge of light from the lantern behind threw his shadow on the wall, short and squat as a gorilla's. His glasses gleamed. Somewhere on his fat person he had an ice pick.

Cowboy must have gone to the levers because in a few seconds the doors smashed shut.

"Hey!" Priest yelled, leaping back outside. "You almost got me."

If only! I thought. If only the door had closed and squashed him like a fat, black bug.

Cowboy had taken Biddy's flashlight with him, and I saw first the long, dark shapes of his legs moving under the poncho. He looked into Biddy's cell and then into mine. "Comfortable?" he asked.

Neither Biddy nor I answered.

"What now?" Priest and Maxie turned to Cowboy for orders. He was the boss man. The king of the Outlaws.

"You'll stay here," Cowboy said. "Maxie and me'll go look for Bean. I get a bad feeling when one of us is missing."

"Aw, Cowboy!" Maxie's eyes flickered into Biddy's cell. "Let me stay. I'll keep Red company. You can take your time."

"Priest stays," Cowboy said.

Priest smiled. "I'll keep Danny-Boy company. And you can still take your time."

Cowboy aimed the flashlight down Broadway. When he and Maxie moved they were instantly out of my line of sight. I slunk back as far as I could get in the cell, fearful of what Priest would do to me, not being able to imagine.

Priest ran the point of the ice pick in a metallic

clink-clink-clink along the bars. His hand went instinctively to where the lock would be on an ordinary gate or door, and stopped. I saw the realization hit him, and it hit me at the same time. He couldn't get in to me. He should have done it before the others left, if he really wanted to keep me company. Now he'd have to go to the lever to open the door and when he did, I'd be gone. Biddy too, because these guys didn't know you could open the doors singly, and were too dumb to figure it out.

I let my breath go and slid down into the corner. How long would it take them to find Jelly Bean? When they did, they'd be back. Then there'd be three of them to work the doors, three of them to work on us. And by that time they'd know what I'd done to Jelly Bean. Stupid they were, but they'd have no trouble seeing my footprints on the wood above where Jelly Bean had fallen. Priest would be shut in with me. Maxie with Biddy. I felt the shakes starting in my legs, moving up till even my teeth were rattling.

"Biddy," I said loudly. "Can you hear me?"

"Yes."

"Are you all right?"

Priest thumped on the bars. "No talking."

"Listen," I said to Biddy. "What if we yell together, real loud? Would the watchman hear us?"

"I don't think so." Biddy's voice was spooky, hollow in the emptiness around us.

Priest stuck his fat face against the bars. Rage tightened his mouth. "I said no talking. Not one more word!"

"The wind's coming in from the city," Biddy went on as if she hadn't heard him. "It'll blow all sounds in the other direction. Besides, the ranger hut's so far away. And I bet Maybelline has her music on. Bach. Loud. She won't hear a thing."

"Okay. But what about the night watchman?"

"Maybelline is the night watchman. The watch woman," Biddy said.

I groaned.

"A watch woman?" Priest laughed his big, roly-poly laugh which sounded fine as long as you couldn't see the coldness of his lizard eyes. "It's some old broad who's the watchman on this place? What a joke! And no gun! We've got nothing to worry about, that's for sure."

But my heart was sinking fast. I'd thought there were two people here who could rescue us. Now I'd discovered there was only one. A woman. I'm all for women. But I'd been hoping for a hard-core muscle builder type.

"Maybelline!" Priest hummed happily. In a few minutes he began pacing up and down, his shadow sliding ahead of him in the cold glow of the lantern. He came and went in front of me. I could hear his footsteps and it seemed to me that each time he paced a little farther. After a while I heard nothing and I guessed he'd gone all the way through the sally port to the door and was peering down the path. I went to my bars and whispered, "Biddy?"

She was right there, almost next to me.

"The guy they went looking for? Jelly Bean? He's hurt real bad. He tried to get me and I kicked him off the ladder. He's lying under the water tower."

"Good. That takes care of one of them."

"Yeah. But I think his leg's busted. I want them to find him, but then again I don't. You know?"

There was a pause and then Biddy said, "I know. Look, he'll be found tomorrow when the tours come. Don't waste your time worrying about him. We have to think about us. Danny? It is Danny, isn't it?"

"Yeah," I said.

"Do you have a watch?"

"No."

"Well, it's eight thirty now. At about ten, Maybelline's going to come up here. She goes all around, checking the place out, and they may not see her coming even if they're on the lookout. There's a back way — she doesn't have to come up the path. Just before ten, we've got to make a lot of noise. Till then we'll have to hold out. Somehow."

"If she misses you, won't she come sooner?"

"She won't miss me. She doesn't even know I'm here. Sometimes one of us stays over with her if we're on duty in the morning. But I didn't tell her I was staying this time."

I remembered. Maybelline was to have been surprised.

"*Did* anybody else stay?"

"No. I just thought I could scare these creeps into letting us go by telling them that. That was before I knew them."

"They don't scare easy," I said.

We stood with our faces against the cages. When I rolled my eyes and stuck my head as far as I could I was able to see her fingers wrapped around the bars. I thought about the men who'd been locked up here before me, doing this same thing, trying to get a glimpse of the person next to them.

Then the cells across Broadway would have been filled too, filled with men staring across the space at the prisoners opposite them, day after day, week after week, year after year. Looking at each other washing in that crummy little basin, sitting on the toilet, raging frantically around the cells, weeping maybe. There was nowhere to hide. Nowhere to be. I couldn't stand it, for them — for us.

"Here comes the black beetle," Biddy whispered. "Danny, I'll give you some kind of sign when it's time."

We moved away from each other as Priest came back.

"What's keeping them?" he asked petulantly.

"Maybe Maybelline got them," Biddy said. "Then there'll just be you, you little crumb."

"Shut up." Priest really liked those two words. "You won't be chirping like that when we get through with you."

He stood there and smiled, and I tried not to look at his smile or think about why he was smiling. And I'd gotten Biddy into this. It was all my fault. Right from the beginning.

Priest was still smiling and picking at a zit by the corner of his mouth. He slid a couple of steps sideways to stare at me. "Now you, Danny-Boy, you'll be all mine. The trouble is, I can't decide what to do with you. One thing I can tell you, though, whatever it is, you won't like it."

"You have to get to me first, creepo," I croaked, pleased that I could speak at all through my fear.

"I'll get to you," he said. "We'll get to both of you. It's only a matter of time."

He switched on Maxie's radio and leaned against the opposite cages, his eyes magnified by the light and the thickness of his glasses. One hand held the ice pick. The other played with the zit. Grace Slick's high, nasal whine came from the black box and when it ended there was some kind of group, the Kinks, I think.

"Nice music," Biddy said. "Suits you."

"Shut up," Priest told her, and we did. There wasn't anything left to say.

CHAPTER

Someone had scratched something into the wall of my cell. Maybe it was done by a prisoner, long ago, or maybe by one of the Indians. Indians had taken possession of the island for a while in the sixties. It was during the Vietnam War, when I guess a lot of people were having demonstrations about a lot of things. Theirs had something to do with Indian land rights. It had all happened just after I was born. But sometimes there was still something about it in the *Chronicle*. The Indians hadn't stayed long. Who'd want to stay long in a place like this?

I could read only some of the words in the cone

of light from Priest's lantern, and for some reason it seemed important to read them all. I ran my fingers over the letters, feeling them. HELP! I AM BEING HELD PRISONER AGAINST MY WILL. I stood thinking about the convict etching out the words. How long had it taken him? How had he managed to hide them? Scratching and scratching, only his sense of humor keeping him alive. What was that saying? Where there's life, there's hope.

I didn't know what we had to hope for here. That Maybelline would hear us and have enough sense to beat it fast back down to her ranger hut and call the cops. That Cowboy and Maxie would meet with a fatal accident. That they wouldn't find Jelly Bean.

When Priest padded away a small distance, I used the grungy toilet in the corner, feeling around its crusty rim so I'd hit the right place in the half dark. Yuk! I tried not to splash in case Biddy would hear. Dumb really to care about that now. But I couldn't help it.

Thoughts hung in my head like sleeping bats. My father. We didn't even know how long the terrorists had held him. He'd been working for a North American oil company in South America when he disappeared. Mom said it was terrible, because nobody could find out what had happened to him. They figured they had him locked up somewhere, and were holding him as a possible hostage. Two years after he disappeared, his body was found. I guess they couldn't even tell for sure how long he'd been dead. Maybe he'd been in a cell like this for those two years. Maybe in one that was even worse.

They flew his body home. I was only seven then, but I remembered everything about the funeral. It was just before Thanksgiving. I remembered the two men in their dark suits who shook my mother's hand and then mine. She told me they were from the State Department. We'd stood on the cemetery hill, with the wind blowing cold the way it can in San Francisco, and I'd looked down and seen Alcatraz through the mist.

Mom and Gran had cried, but I hadn't. I remembered thinking that crying would have seemed fake. I hadn't known my father. Not the way they did. But the tears had come anyway, just at the end, when I'd looked up and seen my mother's face.

Now here I sat in the corner of this freezing cell, my jeans sticking wet to my legs, the music that wasn't music still coming from Maxie's box, making my teeth hurt. I was looking across the space at Priest and thinking about my dad. Priest had a faraway look on his face and I wondered what he was thinking. I was glad I didn't know. It must have been the cold that was making me shake so hard. *Help, somebody, help! I am being held prisoner against my will.*

Priest moved suddenly and clicked off the radio and took the lantern. "I'll be back," he said. "Don't go anywhere." And he slithered away, leaving us in the blackest of blackness. I could hardly see to get across to the bars.

"Biddy?"

I heard her voice right next to me. "I'm here."

"What time is it?"

"Around nine."

I couldn't believe it. I'd only been in this cell for about an hour, and it felt like a couple of years. I'm sorry, Dad. That's an insult to you. I have no understanding of what it would be like to be here for a couple of years. I guess I have no understanding of how it was for you.

Biddy's voice was a whisper that slid through the darkness.

"Danny? I have an idea. When Cowboy and the other one come back I'm going to try to get them — "

"Sh!" I interrupted her. "Priest could be close. Listening. He could have switched off the light and crept back just to hear anything we say. I can't see a thing. Can you?"

"Not much."

We stood, letting our eyes adjust. Gradually the black became lighter. I could see, high above the center aisle, way above the third tier of cells, the pale glimmer of ceiling. That was all.

"You'll know," Biddy whispered at last. "You'll know when I do it."

I'd better know.

It was then that I saw a small shifting of shadow in the cell opposite. A trace of movement, and I whispered aloud, "Rats!" Well, sure there'd be rats in a place like this; there'd have to be. But that one looked big as a rabbit. Then I heard a "miaow" and I remembered the cat. I was just about to say something to Biddy when I saw Priest coming back. The lantern glowed white ahead of him.

"I guess we gave him credit for more brains than he's got," Biddy said.

Yeah, I thought. Or maybe even *he* has brains enough to know that whatever we plan or plot is meaningless anyway. We're caught. But I didn't say that out loud. Things were bad enough. Besides, something was bugging me, something that I needed to think about. Something to do with the cat.

I watched for it in the coming brightness and got a fast glimpse of its black sleekness, its fierce glowing eyes. Then it was gone, springing toward the back of the cell.

"Having a good time?" Priest asked and settled himself again against the opposite cell door.

I stood for a long time, waiting for the cat to reappear, but it never did. Then I crouched in the back corner and tried to think.

The cells across the aisle were locked. A cat could squeeze through the bars. No trouble. A cat can get through anything that's as wide as its whiskers — that's some kind of rule. Maybe it got in that way, but it didn't get out that way or I would have seen it. Of course, it might be sleeping somewhere by the rear wall. But I didn't think so. That cat wasn't in a sleeping mood. No, I was sure it had gone. How?

And then my heart was beating in earnest, big rattling beats, like a train on a loose track. I saw Ranger Rick again, standing on the platform that was outside my cage door. I heard his voice:

"The concrete at the back of the cell's softened with age. The authorities were afraid the prisoners could dig through it and escape. A few did." And this was . . . how many years later? Twenty . . . twenty-five? I remembered the wall in the morgue crumbling away under my fingers. *Oh God, oh please,* I prayed. The words were becoming a litany, a charm that I said over and over again inside my head.

I stared out at Priest. He had turned on the music again and was sitting, legs spread out, ice pick tapping against one knee. He was looking at Biddy. At least I thought that was what he was doing. I edged my hands behind me and began to feel along the back wall. I scraped at it with my fingernails. It felt rock solid.

"What do you think you're doing?"

My heart somersaulted. I stood up, stammering, and then saw that Priest was looking at Biddy, not me.

"What does it look like I'm doing?" Biddy asked. "Hang gliding? I'm cleaning out my pockets to see if by any chance I have a lethal weapon that I could use on you. Unfortunately, I can't seem to find one."

Priest pointed. "What's that?"

"This?" I realized she must be holding something up. "A book. Haven't you ever seen a book before?"

Priest grinned. "Yeah. But all the people I know carry those kinds of weapons you were talking about. Not books."

Biddy had been reading a book on the boat when I'd first seen her. This must be the one. I remembered the three beautiful women on the cover. I couldn't recall the title and I didn't care. All that mattered was that Priest wasn't watching me. I turned and poked my fingers frantically along the wall, down where it met the floor. Tight, tight and firm, without even a crack.

"Pass it out here," Priest said. I could see his bulky side as he walked to Biddy's cell, one thick, black leg, one cruddy black-laced shoe, the kind nobody else would be caught dead in.

He retreated again, carrying the book, and I moved and sat in the other corner with my hands in back of me. My fingers searched the angle made by the wall between the cells, feeling for a weak spot.

"What's the book about?" Priest asked. "Are these a bunch of hot broads? Would I like them?"

"I'll tell you one thing for sure," Biddy said. "They wouldn't like you."

My fingers had stopped, not daring to believe what they'd found. The cement was loose here, dropping in soft little chunks no bigger than crumbs as I touched it. They made a little sound when they hit the floor and I coughed to cover it.

"Shut up," Priest bellowed. He had his litany and I had mine, and I was repeating mine over and over as my fingers probed. I'd made a hole now, as big around as a cigarette. One finger got through to the space on the other side. I wiggled it ecstatically.

Priest was reading out loud from about halfway through the book. "He was looking at her *in . . . in . . . intently*" As he stammered the word he looked to Biddy for approval.

"Wonderful," she said. "Is there no end to your talents?"

"He was looking at her in . . . tently and suddenly she felt for an in . . . instant a cold shiv . . shiver pass through her. It wasn't the chill of *for . . . for . . .*"

Priest stopped again, mouthing the word.

"Spell it." Biddy's voice dripped sarcasm and I closed my eyes and begged, *Biddy, Biddy, don't put him off, don't make him mad, don't stop him. I'm working in here.*

"F-O-R-B-O-D-I-N-G."

Priest read on. It was as if he were in the second grade and had to stumble over every word, but this wasn't a second-grade book and he was enjoying it. He wasn't enjoying Biddy's hoots of laughter, though. *Stop it, Biddy*, I thought. *Stop it.* After a few minutes Priest said nastily: "Here. You read it," and he stuffed the book back through the bars to Biddy. I sat quietly, my best chance gone. Now I'd have to try again with my hands behind my back and no leverage. I'd remembered the little nail clippers in my pocket and I was using the point of the click-out file to chip at the harder cement around the hole.

"Read out loud," Priest said. "I'm bored waiting for those guys." He sat back, his eyes riveted on Biddy as she read.

" 'I don't see why a girl has to quit her job just because she gets married,' Caroline said. 'I'd like to keep mine. It's really more of a career to me than a job. I like it.'

" 'Maybe you'll marry Paul,' Kippie said comfortably.

" 'I haven't even laid eyes on him yet!'

" 'You'll like him. He's sweet. He always kisses me good-bye.' "

Priest stopped her. "Who is this Kippie? Who are they talking about? Is she one of the dolls on the front?"

"No. I think Caroline is."

I was blessing Biddy and dumb old Priest and Kippie and Caroline and praying, keep going, Biddy, keep him occupied. She did.

Words flowed around me. I had two fingers

through the hole now, and I'd wadded the old Kleenex from my pocket below the droppings, to muffle whatever sound they made as they fell. What if I poked a hole big enough to wriggle through? For the very first time I was glad to be small. It only needed to be as wide as my whiskers, I thought hysterically. It's a law. Where my whiskers can get through I can get through.

My fingers were bleeding. I could feel the dust from the cement sticking to their rawness. The skin was scraped from my knuckles too. My knuckles! Who cared? The skin would be scraped from more than that, if I couldn't get us out of here.

Biddy's voice came from the next cell.

" 'I remember our freshman year when you first started to shave your legs,' Caroline said. 'I was kind of shocked for some reason.'

Priest tittered.

I could get my whole arm through the hole now. The cement was coming away in pebbles, not crumbs. I stopped and began to ease off my jacket. I needed more padding in case Priest heard the pebbles fall.

His eyes shifted from Biddy to me. "What're you doing?"

"Taking off my coat," I said. "I'm warm."

"Warm? It's freezing in here."

"I thought I'd lie down," I said and I arranged the jacket in front of the hole, like a pillow, and curled myself with my back to the light, thankful that he couldn't get in to check. But he didn't seem worried.

"Read more," he told Biddy.

I waited a few seconds till I was sure it was safe to start prodding again. Then I heard the soft pad of footsteps and I froze.

Priest's head turned and he said in an aggrieved voice, "What took you guys? I thought you'd started swimming for shore."

I followed his gaze and saw the small, bouncing ball of light coming toward us. Cowboy and Maxie were back.

CHAPTER

"Did you find Bean?" Priest asked.

"No."

My stomach unclenched. That nice, sunken-in nest had hidden Jelly Bean from the path. Thank you, God.

"We searched the whole damn island. But there's a million places he could be."

Maxie's eyes, like Cowboy's, were fixed on something in Biddy's cell. It wasn't hard to figure out what. I was the reason they'd come to Alcatraz. But now they had her. I might still be Priest's main interest, but I sure wasn't theirs.

Maxie put the music back on. "You know Bean," he said. "He's always off, poking that long nose of his into something."

"Forget about Bean for now." It had to be raining hard outside. Water dripped from Cowboy's big hat and ran in puddles from the bottom of the poncho. His hair hung sleek and straight, so that he looked more like Cochise or Geronimo than any Cowboy. "We'll check again later. Bean's got to learn he can't go messing around on his own like that."

"Remember in the parking lot that time, when we were going to jump the Gomez sisters, and he was supposed to wait outside the elevators and..." Priest began.

Cowboy turned his stare on him. "I said, forget Bean for now." He took off his hat, shook it and put it back on again.

"Hey!" Priest said. "You know the watchman's some old girl called Mabel or something? Can you beat it?"

Maxie giggled and reached out to make the music louder. "We watched her for a while through the windows. Silly looking old bag. She's sitting there, playing cards with herself and listening to some cruddy high-balling music. Big old broad, built like a trolley car."

"Maybe you shoulda brought her up here," Priest said. "We coulda partied."

Cowboy's voice was cold. "Don't be stupid. She can't know we're here. Tomorrow we leave on the first boat back. Nobody knows. Nobody hassles us."

"I'll know," Biddy said sharply and I thought, be quiet, Biddy, just be quiet.

Cowboy smiled and I saw his big, gravestone teeth. "Sure you'll know, honey-baby. But you won't tell."

"I won't, if you let us go now," Biddy said. "I won't say a word."

"And if we don't let you go now?" The eyes under the hat brim were staring at her, staring.

There was silence and then Biddy said quietly, "I guess I won't tell then either."

I breathed again. Good, Biddy.

I saw Cowboy's face, the shadows under the cheekbones, the broad, fleshy nose. "Yes, you will," he said.

Maxie hopped from one foot to the other, looking in at Biddy, up at Cowboy, over at me, up and down and round and round, his eyes rolling like dice.

"Maybe she doesn't understand, Cowboy," Maxie said. "Tell her what'll happen to her if she talks. How it'll be a lot worse than tonight. None of the other girls ever told. Maybe she doesn't understand."

Cowboy nodded as if he'd just made a decision. "She understands. But she's not like the others. She'll tell." His head flicked toward my cell. "Danny-

94

Boy, now, he wouldn't tell. But he's with her."

I'd never been so scared in my life. It wasn't hard to figure the way Cowboy was thinking. They'd leave in the morning on the first boat. But where would we be? Someplace where we wouldn't tell. Someplace like the bottom of the bay. Who'd know I'd ever been on Alcatraz? No one. And I imagined what people would say about Biddy: "Wasn't it awful about that National Park Ranger who disappeared the other night? One of the other rangers said she'd planned on staying over on the island all night. Something to do with a birthday. Pretty foolish of her. But nowadays these young people think they can do anything. She must have fallen off one of the cliffs into the sea. Too bad. Really, really sad."

I could see the two bodies being fished from the water, probably miles apart, with nothing to connect them. The way the ocean currents ran, Biddy might be pulled in from Sausalito and me from Half Moon Bay. I didn't think the Outlaws had ever killed anyone. But I knew they could, if they had to. In a way, we were all in a trap. Biddy and I couldn't escape. They couldn't let us escape.

I retreated to the back of the cell, sat down with my hands behind me and dug feverishly at the hole. I was as breathless as if I'd run a million miles.

Maxie turned the stereo sound up. There was something wordless playing, something with a beat like African drums, and he was moving with it, shimmying, sometimes where I could see him, sometimes out of my view. His legs seemed boneless, letting him down low like a guy trying to wriggle under a fence without touching the wire, then bringing him up again. And his eyes were on Biddy wherever he moved, peering back at her over his shoulder, watching her from the crook of his elbow.

Whatever Maxie was doing made my mouth go dry. I rose to my feet and moved over to the door. Something was coming, that I knew. It hung in the cold, stale air like those first faint rumblings of walls and floors and dangling lights before the earthquake hits full force.

"You dance very well," Biddy said. I couldn't believe she was saying that, in that cool, clear voice Why didn't she just keep quiet and not make them notice her any more than they were noticing her already? Why didn't she hold on and pray that the earthquake would pass?

"Oh yeah?" Maxie was spurred on to lower lows, one hand on the ground, one leg going out as he spun like a skater on ice.

"*Very* well," Biddy said.

Priest was swaying from side to side, too, trying to snap his pudgy fingers, grinning his imbecile grin. Only Cowboy stood motionless in the shadow of his wet, black hat.

The music had changed. It was a pulse now, with something terrifying in it.

"Watch this!" Maxie had one arm out, the other against his chest as he leaped and spun. "I bet you're a good dancer too, Red. You like to dance?"

"Sure," Biddy said.

Was she crazy? And then I understood. We'd stood in the dark and she'd said to me 'You'll know.' She hadn't planned this. It had happened and she was taking advantage of it. It would get her out of the cell where maybe she'd have a chance.

"Go open the doors, Priest!" Maxie ordered. His feet were still moving, slithering around on the floor, his elbows and shoulders jerking up and down. "It's okay, isn't it, Cowboy?" he asked, without taking his gaze from Biddy. "It's okay to have some fun?"

My fingers tightened on the bars. Yes or no? It hung in the balance. I didn't want it to be yes . . . for Biddy to go out there and be pawed by these weirdos. But . . . what if she could do something? And what if they kept on dancing, and I got a chance to dig away at my escape hole?

Cowboy was thinking about it.

"No way," Biddy said. "I said I like to dance. I didn't say I'd enjoy it with a toad like you."

"Hey! Hey, honey-baby!" Cowboy's voice was soft and he showed his big, horse teeth. "Don't turn your back on us when we're talking to you! I can see we're going to have to teach you some manners. And if this nice boy here is kind enough to ask you to dance, you'll dance. Open the door, Priest. And stay out there. Keep an eye open for the old broad."

"Aw Cowboy," Priest whined. "I'm sick of watching and hanging around. I want to have some fun too."

"You're going to have fun. Lots of fun. Fun with Danny-Boy. But it's early. There's no need to rush anything. No need for any of us to rush anything. These are just the preliminaries."

Maxie giggled and Cowboy turned his head toward Priest. "Get going."

Priest went at a trot to the end of the cell block. In a minute the doors slid open.

"Just move back, Danny-Boy," Cowboy said. "It's not your turn yet. And you, honey-baby, you move forward."

She must have hung back because Cowboy took a quick step and yanked her from behind the bars. The doors slammed again, leaving me on the inside, her on the outside.

Biddy had pressed herself tight against the closed door of her cell, but I'd never been as certain of anything as I was of this. She was exactly where she wanted to be. She'd played it right, knowing that if she hung back they'd make her come out. If she'd been eager, Cowboy would have kept her inside.

"Dance!" Cowboy said, and he yanked her forward again.

Now Maxie was writhing toward her, and Cowboy was dancing too, both of them facing Biddy like a pair of wild, dark birds, strutting to attract the female.

Biddy's face was white. Her hair gathered all the light from the lantern and held it, trapped in its own redness. Neither Cowboy nor Maxie had touched her yet, and I wanted to move back, to get on with what I should be doing, had to do. But I couldn't. I was hypnotized. There was no way I could tear myself away from the bars. They'd jiggled out of my sight now, but I could hear their movements, the ragged sound of breathing that pulsed through the music.

Then I heard Cowboy whisper. "Take off that jacket, honey-baby. Can't dance with a jacket like that on."

I heard the hiss of a zipper and then I saw Maxie's arm holding the green ranger coat. He swung it the way the striptease artist that Curt and I had snuck in to see at the Pussycat had swung her long, white gloves, before she threw them into the audience. The jacket landed against the bars of the other cells.

I jammed my head against my cage so I could see. I wanted to be out there with them. I wanted to be dancing with Biddy. All the strange, hurting needs that I'd been havihg filled me and overflowed. Oh, Biddy, you're so beautiful!

She was moving backward, swinging with the music and Cowboy swayed down to meet her. He didn't move the way Maxie did, flapping and swirling. Only his feet and his lower half were alive, the rest of him was stiff, and straight. But there was grace in him and some kind of fierce power, like a cobra rising heavy-headed from the snake charmer's basket.

Now Maxie was whirling up to grab Biddy's hand, to throw her back at arm's length, to pull her again so she bumped against him. "Oh, you're nice," he whispered. "Real nice."

As he swung her back, her lifeless face turned toward me again and one arm came up in a dreamy sort of arc, and then ... then ... for a second her finger brushed the face of her watch.

Relief made me dizzy. She wasn't in a trance. She wasn't sleepwalking. Oh Biddy! Biddy! It's time. And you know exactly what you're doing.

As she passed the black box on its wooden platform, Biddy stopped, hips still swaying, eyes closed, and turned the hard, gritty music higher.

Cowboy swung back beside her. He still wore his hat and his long dark poncho, and I saw his hand close on her wrist and I thought he was going to swing her out, the way Maxie had done. But he didn't. He was holding her, and they were both suddenly still. He reached behind him and the music fell into silence.

"It was loud enough," he said.

Biddy's voice faltered. "I couldn't hear. I like that song."

"You could hear."

Maxie still twitched to the remembered music. "Hey, man! What did you turn it off for?" He was behind Biddy, his hands sliding over her shoulders, down her arms. "I sure do like you a lot," he murmured.

Cowboy grabbed his arm. "Listen, you moron! Little Miss Ranger's smart. She's cooking something." His voice raised. "Priest! Open the doors. Then get down here."

The bars rasped apart.

"Watch him," Cowboy said. The "him" was me. I didn't need watching. I couldn't have moved if I'd wanted to.

Priest hulked down the aisle. "What? You ready for me to do Danny-Boy now?" He hulked into my cell.

"Watch him, that's all." Cowboy's full concentration was on Biddy. "You!" he said. "Tell us."

"I don't know what you ..." Biddy began.

Cowboy grabbed a fistful of her hair.

"Like to dance, do you?" he asked. "Like us too?" I felt his rage. It was going to be worse for her, because she'd messed with him. She'd fooled the King. She'd made him think she was getting off on him. He was mad enough to kill her right now.

I slithered a little to the side and Priest snatched my hair the way Cowboy had taken Biddy's. He held the point of the ice pick at my throat. "Oh, I'd love to take care of you, Danny-Boy. I'm just waiting for the word." He would love to. I sensed the excitement coming from him. He'd see Biddy hurt first, and then he'd get to hurt me.

"I'm going to ask each question once, honey-baby," Cowboy said. "And you're going to answer once. Fast. The woman comes up here every night, doesn't she?"

"Yes," Biddy gasped.

"She's coming any minute, right?"

"Yes." Her eyes were watering.

"Does she have a big lantern?"

"Yes. But . . . you have it."

"She'll use a flashlight then?"

"Yes."

Cowboy let her go and straightened. "Priest, take Danny-Boy to the back of the cell. Hold him facing the wall." The lantern went off.

Priest shoved me ahead of him in the darkness, pushing my nose against the dusty concrete. I sensed a faint lifting of the blackness. Cowboy's heavy steps passed our cell.

"All right," he said. "I've tried it out. Unless she

shines her light into each cell she won't see us. Not if we're back against the wall."

Priest gave my head a last thump before we turned around. "I can show you somewhere we could go," he told Cowboy. "I found it. There's cells with no bars. Just big old heavy doors. She'd never find us."

I knew where he meant. I'd been in one of those cells. If Cowboy put us in there, we'd never get out. They were black holes. Black holes of horror.

"No. We might walk into her. Maybe she even feels her way around this place, she knows it so well."

"What if she walks into Bean?" Maxie giggled. "Then she'll not walk into nothin' no more."

The flashlight touched each of our faces, stopping on Biddy's. "I'm guessing, honey-baby," Cowboy whispered. "If I'm wrong, you'd better speak up. I'm guessing sometimes the doors are closed at the end of the tour and sometimes they're left open. Right?"

Biddy's throat moved as she swallowed. "Yes," she whispered.

Cowboy smiled. I could see the rage had died in him. He was Mr. Cool again, king of the Outlaws. "We'll leave them open. They make too much noise."

"Maxie, you go in with Danny-boy. Priest, you take her."

"Come on, Cowboy, give her to me!" Maxie leaned from behind Biddy and licked the side of her neck. I saw her shudder.

"I want no problems," Cowboy said. "Do what I tell you."

Biddy stumbled for the cell before anyone could touch her. Cowboy threw her jacket after her. "Hide that book and the radio, Priest."

I went to the back wall, far away from the hole my jacket was hiding. Maxie was still wriggling inside his clothes. I smelled the sweat on him. He stank like a dog that had just come in from the rain.

Cowboy's voice was behind us. "One sound," he said, "one breath out of you and you're all dead. That means the old watchwoman too, honey-baby, whether it spoils our plans or not." I sensed his smile again, the pulling of the lips across those big, gravestone teeth. "Trust me." The flashlight went out.

Maxie's arm circled my waist, pushing me against the wall. I knew the knife was in his other hand. I can't remember ever feeling as scared as I did standing there in that pitch black cell, with Maxie squirming and twitching beside me.

C H A P T E R

10

There was silence, but there was no silence. Small sounds came from the old prison. Creakings, echoes, shufflings. Far, far away in another world a foghorn uttered its mournful cry. These must be the sounds Al Capone had heard at night. And the Bird Man. And Machine Gun Kelly. My nose was filled with dust and the smell of Maxie. I sneezed.

"Don't do that again, kid," Maxie breathed. I hoped I wouldn't do it again, but how do you stop a sneeze if it's coming? With Maxie at your back you stop it.

My raw hands felt as if they'd been stung by a

hundred bees. I wanted to blow on them, but I didn't dare move.

I thought about Biddy in there with Priest and felt sick.

Suppose Maybelline's flashlight has a stronger beam than Cowboy's, dim as his is with tonight's use? Suppose she sees more than he thought she'd see? If she does, poor Maybelline. I heard a small, questioning miaow. The cat was back.

Now there was a new sound ... footsteps ... footsteps echoing somewhere in emptiness, coming closer ... stopping. And then, incredibly, the ear shattering crash of all the cell doors all the way along our row clanking shut.

My head reeled. Maybelline had locked us in! I couldn't get hold of the thought. What did it mean to us? Suppose Cowboy was in one of the cells too? We'd all be trapped, them and us. What would happen then? I should call, scream, yell at Maybelline. But Cowboy might be right behind her.

Maxie's hand was over my mouth and he was at my back now, mashing me against the wall, whispering, "Don't even squeak, Danny-Boy."

The heavy feet marched along Broadway. I rolled my eyes to the side and saw the yellow beam of light coming toward us. It seemed bright as day to me, and I saw that the light was tracking from left to right. Maybelline was shining it into each cell, doing it by the book, or whatever.

I picked up my litany again. *Oh God, oh please!* Please what? Let Maybelline see us? Yes, but as soon as you do, Maybelline, run! Get away from Cowboy!

Were the feet slowing even more? Yes! And now they'd stopped.

Maxie's hand tightened on my mouth and I felt the jiggling of his body against mine. Then there was a woman's voice, right outside our cell.

"Puss ... Puss ... come out here!"

I jerked my head, making little grunting noises. Before Maxie squashed me to the wall again, I saw her. She was a dark figure behind her flashlight, crouched down, her back to us. And I knew what she was doing. The cat had gone back to its cell across the aisle. She was coaxing it out.

"There now!" Her shoes scuffed as she got up, letting out a whoosh of heavy breath. "Pretty Valentine. You want your supper? A birthday supper for both of us? Sardines? Hm? Don't scratch. If you don't want sardines, you don't have to have them. All the more for me."

The footsteps were moving on. I shut my eyes in frustration, imagining Maybelline bent over the cat, cradling it, shining her good bright light again from side to side. Dumb cat — dumb, stupid cat! Maybelline mightn't have seen us anyway, but it felt good to turn my anger on the animal.

A gate clanged. Then there was only the prison

creaking around us, the little slow slidings and mumblings of the old shifting stones. Ten o'clock had come and gone. Ten o'clock had gone forever.

Maxie let me go and I moved out from the wall. It was so dark that I could see only the blacker blackness of his body. His shape moved to the bars. "Priest?"

"Yeah?"

"We're locked in." What a lame brain! Did he think Priest didn't know?

"I know," Priest said. Lame brain number two.

"Biddy?" I called, but it was Priest who answered. "Shut up."

"Biddy? Are you okay?"

"She's okay," Priest said. Why wasn't she answering me herself?

"Did you hurt her, you creep?" I croaked.

"She ain't hurt. She's just . . . resting."

Maxie giggled. "Resting?"

I grabbed at the bars. Resting?

Maxie was rattling the doors of the cage now. "Hey, how do we get out of here? Cowboy!" he yelled. "Cowboy!"

No one answered.

"Maybe he's locked in too," I said and Maxie rattled the door harder.

"He's watching the old girl, that's what it is. He'll stay with her till it's safe to let us out." But Maxie's voice was unsure.

"I'll bet he is locked in," I said again. "Then we'll all be here till they let us out in the morning."

"Naw," Maxie said, uncertainly, and added, "Shut up." Maxie liked Priest's favorite words, too.

I retreated, close to the hole in the concrete. If only Maxie didn't find it. If only it were wider. I put my hands behind and felt around it. It was about as big as a football, with jagged edges. I didn't dare pick at it. How big would it have to be for me to get through?

Maxie was sitting too. I could see his shadowy shape close to the bars and hear him fidgeting around.

Priest's voice came through the wall. "Geez! I hate being locked up like this. You think Cowboy'll get us out all right?"

"Shut up, Priest! Just shut up!" Maxie yelled.

What was Biddy doing? Maybe she'd fainted. Bull! Girls didn't faint anymore, especially girls like Biddy. More likely she was plotting something, figuring what we could do next. I wouldn't be surprised if she'd known all along that Maybelline would close the doors. I was filled with admiration for her. But I wished I knew that she was all right.

Maxie picked my thoughts out of the air. "Is the girl okay, Priest?" he shouted. "Did she give you any trouble?"

"She's okay." Priest sounded disgusted. "She was gonna yell. She bit my hand. I had to bang her head against the wall, but she's okay."

"Danny? Danny?" A little voice. Hard to hear her. "I'm all right. It's just a bump."

I wrapped my arms tight about myself. So Priest had banged her head on the wall! He liked to do that. He'd banged mine too. He was strong and powerful and everyone was scared of him, partly because he always carried that rotten ice pick. Without it he'd be just a fat little creep. If I ever, ever got the chance I was going to give Priest a bump he'd never forget.

"So shut up then, if you're all right," Priest said.

"You too," Maxie ordered me.

I slumped in front of my hole. We were all waiting, waiting for Cowboy. Somehow I knew he was loose and he'd be back to get us. Cowboy wouldn't let himself be caught in any trap. King of the Out laws. King of the cobras. He'd be back.

It seemed a long time. My mind drifted. Mom and Gran would be freaked out by now. They'd probably called the cops and given them a description of me. "Fourteen, but small for his age. No, he's not the kind of kid to run away. No he's never been in any trouble." Maybe they'd cry, the way they cried at my dad's funeral. It wasn't fair. Mom and Gran had had enough. Me too, come to think of it.

Maxie was pacing the cell now. He leaned against the walls, pulling his knees up and down. "There's something written here." His fingers traced the letters in the concrete.

"Help," I said. "I am being held prisoner against my will."

Maxie grunted. "I don't get it. Who did he think was going to help him?" He raised his voice. "Are you asleep, Priest?"

"Are you kidding? Who could sleep in a freezing hole like this?"

I thought about Jelly Bean for some reason. I couldn't believe I'd ever worried that he might die. Then I thought about Biddy in there, probably as scared as I was.

"Hey!" Maxie was at the bars again. "Here he comes!"

Cowboy came down Broadway with the lantern and peered into each cell in turn. "Well," he said. "Four little birds in two little cages." His thin smile stretched his lips. "You'll be glad to know the old woman's down in her little hut, all snug and secure. But I think I'll just leave you where you are for a while longer. You can think over your sins, Maxie. Meditate, like those weirdos with the skinheads and the orange robes."

"Come on, Cowboy, stop foolin' around and let us out."

Cowboy smiled some more. "You want out? Don't like it in jail? Maybe it'll make you mend your ways, Maxie. See where a life of crime gets you?"

He'd moved to Priest's and Biddy's cell. "Aw, honey-baby, you look all shook up. Did Priest make that ugly old bump on your head? Shame on you, Priest."

"Come on, Cowboy! Cut the bull and get us out of here!"

"Well," Cowboy seemed to consider, but he was already walking toward the levers.

Maxie and Priest were gone in a flash as soon as the doors slid apart. I stayed on the floor, hiding my creep hole. I think an opening has to be big enough to let your head through if you're a person. My head was still a lot bigger than that football-sized space. And what about my shoulders? I figured there was probably a way to get them through one at a time.

The three Outlaws had moved a few steps away and were talking in whispers. The doors were still open, but I knew there was no way to rush them or to outrun them.

Priest trotted off toward the end of the cells and Cowboy crooked a finger, first at Biddy and then at me. "Come out, little birds. It's exercise time."

Oh, no, I thought. If I move they'll see the hole. There's no way they can miss it. And if I don't move they'll come and drag me out, and then they'll see it for sure.

Cowboy was looking into Biddy's cell.

I got up and out quickly, while the lantern shone into her cell instead of mine.

The four of us stood in the glow of Cowboy's lantern. There was a lump close to Biddy's right eye. I wished I could help her. I tried to smile, but I wasn't sure if it was convincing.

Exercise time, Cowboy had said. What did he mean by that?

And then Priest's voice came leaping excitedly down Broadway. "Cowboy! Cowboy! Here's Jelly Bean."

Biddy's frightened eyes met mine. "Oh no . . . how could he?" she whispered. And I was thinking the same thing because I'd seen him lying in the grass and . . . Suddenly I saw Cowboy's face, the eyes watching, watching, and then I knew. Jelly Bean wasn't coming. It was a trick, and it had worked. Priest appeared, small and squat as a spider at the end of the aisle.

Every bit of Cowboy was stiff with rage. The tight voice came through his tight lips. "You were surprised there, weren't you, little Miss Ranger. And why was that? I think it was because you know where Bean is. Because you didn't think he'd come walking up that path. Because you *knew* he wouldn't. And how did you know? Because you took care of him, somehow, before we met up with you, smart little ranger girl." Cowboy's fists were clenched, and I knew that I couldn't let anything happen to Biddy . . . not again.

I leaped forward. "She didn't do anything. She doesn't know. I'm the one who knows. I'll tell you."

Maxie hooted. "You? Naw! You'd never have the guts."

Priest was shouting along the aisle. "How did I do, Cowboy? Did I do good?"

"You did great. Good as Al Pacino. Stay up there, Priest. I'm going to need you some more." Cowboy stared down at me. "Okay, Danny-Boy. Where's Jelly Bean?

"He's foolin' you," Maxie said. "He doesn't know."

Cowboy grabbed my ear. "Where?"

I swallowed.

"I'm waiting. But I'm not waiting much longer."

I tried to make the bats that were fluttering in my head be still. Why didn't I have a story ready? I didn't want them to really find Jelly Bean. They'd know what happened right off.

"He . . . he went into one of those old deserted houses. I was on top of the water tower. I . . . I saw him. He went up the stairs and he fell. The stairs gave way."

Cowboy's stare pierced through to my brain and the bats fluttered in fright.

"What old deserted house?"

"I don't know. Maybe it was the warden's, or the

guards'. The one at the first bend in the road." I spoke quickly. "I think he might have busted his leg. He's lying there behind the wall." I'm no good at lying. I didn't know if they believed me.

"Geez!" Maxie said.

"That dumb head! How're we going to get him out of here with a busted leg?" Cowboy muttered. His laser stare hadn't moved and his voice was so quiet I could hardly hear it. But I did. "You'd better be telling it straight, kid. I hope you know that." He pushed me away. "Get back in the cell. You too, ranger."

We stumbled back through our open doors.

"What're we going to do now, Cowboy?" Maxie asked.

"We're going to see how bad off the Bean is."

"It doesn't need two of us to do that. I'll stay. You go."

"We both go. We might have to lift him. Priest keeps watch on these two."

I stood looking through the bars. Make them both go. I need a chance to dig and prod and try to save us. Please make them both go.

Somebody must have heard me. They both went.

CHAPTER

11

They left the lantern with Priest, though they'd argued about it. "That flashlight's finished. It's going to give out on us," Maxie had said.

"You think we should be shining a lantern down there, close to the ranger hut? You're crazy." Nobody really argued with Cowboy. He made the decisions.

Maxie had wanted to take me. "He can show us. It'll save time."

My heart did a few wild flip-flops before Cowboy said: "Danny-Boy stays. We'll have our hands full with Bean. You want the kid slipping away from us?"

116

So Cowboy and Maxie went and Priest tagged along after them. "How come I'm always the one left behind?" he whined. "I'm tired of sitting in there, watching those two. There's nothing to do."

I waited till I couldn't hear the voices, only the footsteps getting fainter and fainter.

"Biddy?" I whispered. "I'm digging a hole through the back wall. Watch for Priest. Warn me."

"Danny! A hole! Do you think you can?"

"I'm nearly through. Watch for me. And be careful! He might come without the light."

Then I started to dig again. There was no need to worry too much about noise now that Priest was outside.

My fingers were numb. They'd passed pain; they didn't even seem to belong to me. I wiped their wetness on my jeans. The point on the little nail clippers was bent and blunted now. But it was still better than my bent and blunted fingers. I chipped and chipped.

Either the concrete got harder as the hole widened, or I was getting tired. My touch told me the hole was no bigger than when Cowboy and Maxie had left.

Where were they now? They'd hurry down the road, keeping to the side shadows, slowing as they reached the warden's tumbledown house. They'd move forward in the dark, saving what was left of the flashlight. They'd climb through the rubble, turning on their light when they got close to the stairs, searching for Bean. Were the stairs still standing? I didn't know.

How far had they gotten now? How much time had I left before they stormed back? Not much.

If only *I* had the lantern. If only I could see. Sometimes I prodded what I thought was wall and found only air. Often I hacked with the pointed steel at my own searching hand.

Then I remembered Jelly Bean's matches. I took them from my pocket and tried to strike one. My frozen fingers couldn't make it work. Two wasted. Three. Then I got one lit and its small flicker showed me solid looking rock on either side of my hole. I wished I hadn't seen. It was hopeless. I'd never get the hole any bigger.

I wedged one shoulder in. It wouldn't fit. I tried my head. It wouldn't fit either. The rim of concrete pressed against my eyes and cheekbones and chin. Even the cat couldn't get through it.

"Danny! Danny! Priest's coming," Biddy whispered.

I sat down fast, scraping the bits of loosened concrete in a pile behind me, squatting on them like a hen on her eggs as the lantern light came closer and closer. I closed my eyes, slumped against the wall, and pretended to be asleep.

I could sense Priest studying me and then he moved, holding the light on Biddy.

"So what did you think?"

"About what?"

"About me. My acting. Pretty good, huh?"

"Very good," Biddy said.

"It sure fooled you."

"It sure did."

I slitted my eyes and peered out at him. He had slumped himself against the opposite cells again.

"How about reading to me some more?" He grinned in Biddy's direction. "It's boring out here."

I couldn't believe it. I didn't want to believe it. Priest was going to slob there, right opposite us, cutting off our last chance of escape.

Biddy's hand, holding the book, came through the bars. "Read it yourself. I'm not in the mood."

"Well, get in the mood. I like it better when you read to me."

"Forget it. I have a headache. Somebody banged my head on the wall. See this?" She must have touched the bump because Priest grinned. "It hurts to talk, too, so good-bye."

"You'll do what I tell you," Priest said.

Biddy didn't answer.

Thank heaven none of them had discovered that the doors opened singly. It was the one thing that had gone right for us.

Through half-open eyes I saw Priest scowl and walk over to take the book. He opened it at the first page and his lips moved. One pudgy finger ran along the print, stopping every few seconds as he squinted and mouthed.

He slammed the book shut and glared at Biddy. Then he opened the book again, tore out a page, and folded it slowly and carefully, his fat tongue coming out from between his fat lips as he concentrated. He was a retard. A dangerous retard. He had the page folded into a dart now and he aimed along the length of Broadway, throwing high.

The paper airplane sailed up, its nose pointing to the ceiling, and disappeared from my sight. I heard the small plop as it landed. Priest pursed his lips. He tore out another page and began the folding all over again. We were finished! This dummy was going to tear the book apart, page by page.

When Priest liked the way a plane flew, he'd grunt with satisfaction. He tried the extra weight of two pages together while I tried to picture where Cowboy and Maxie were and how soon it would be before they'd be back to massacre me. The two-page planes were a flop. Priest went back to single-page flight. He tried folding the paper along its length, then along its breadth. He made one plane from the back cover and another from the front cover.

Help, help, I thought. I am being held prisoner.

But there was no one to help but me, and I was stuck there, stuck watching Priest playing his imbecile games.

It was a thick book. Three hundred pages, maybe more. Three hundred paper darts. I'd thought once that this was the kind of place where bats would live, coming out at night to dip and swoop and glide. Instead paper bats had come to fly through the emptiness.

One rose, turned in midair and landed in the tier of cells above.

"Hey!" Priest jumped up and clapped his hands. "That was a good one!"

"My kid brother used to make paper airplanes in kindergarten," Biddy said. "Then he got too old. He's seven now."

"You've got a smart mouth, you know it?" Priest thumped her cell door with the tattered book, shaking the loosened pages free to scatter around his feet. He flung what was left of the book in a flutter down the aisle.

Go, go, go away, I pleaded silently.

He sat again, picking at his zit, working it.

"Hey, you!" He was glaring at me now. "Talk to me."

I didn't answer.

He took off his glasses, pulled loose the tail of his cruddy black shirt, used it to shine them. And all the time, my insides were churning.

Go, go go.

Without the glasses his eyes were small and sightless, like dry pebbles. He put the glasses on again blinked around, and scratched at his belly.

Go, go!

He ambled across to Maxie's stereo, picked it up, and left.

I made myself wait.

"I think he's really gone," Biddy whispered.

"Biddy, have you anything I can use for digging?" I whispered. "Try your pockets."

"I've looked already, Danny. There's not a thing. Nothing. How far have you got?"

"It's going good," I lied. "Keep watching."

I got back on my knees in a blackness that seemed blacker than ever. Going good? Who was I kidding? And where were Cowboy and Maxie now? Would they check another house before they came back? Would they think they had the wrong one? Or would they suddenly come roaring down Broadway, spewing fury, knowing I'd lied to them.

I'd lost so much time.

There was a small snap and something tinkled at my feet. The end of my file! It had broken off, leaving me with only a stub. I stood, put my heel against the side of the hole, and pushed. Nothing. I kicked.

"Danny?"

"Don't tell me he's coming back?"

"No. What are you doing now?'

"Don't worry. I'm getting out." I sat in front of the cat-sized hole, exhausted. Finished. It would take a week to make it big enough.

I lit another match. The flame shook itself out in my jumpy hand. Another one. I bent to examine the hole and saw it . . . a crack, a beautiful gaping crack along one side. My poor overworked heart rattled past the speed limit again. I'd never known it could do all these different tricks. The match glowed down to burn my fingers.

I dropped it, stepped back, bent my knee and kicked at the crack with all the strength I had left. There was a groan, a rumble, then a falling. Sweat poured from me.

"Danny?"

"I'm through." I risked another match. Now I had a real hole. There was no time to say more to Biddy. No time to wonder if Priest had heard my small avalanche and was coming. I had to get out. I went at a crawl, head first. My behind stuck, but it pulled free. My legs were through, and I was out. I stood, panting. Bits of concrete dropped like rain from my hair. I spat out grit. Where was I anyway? What if I'd just crawled from one cell into another?

The match I lit showed me a long, dusty corridor that seemed to run the length of the row of cells, directly behind them. There were a couple of old buckets and a dried-up straggle of mop that looked as if it had been standing there for the past twenty years. I thumped once on the back of Biddy's cell as I eased past it. Then I edged along, feeling with my hands on the wall. It moldered, dusty at my touch. There was a faint, faint glow far ahead. The light at the end of the tunnel, I thought crazily.

I slithered forward, through cobwebs that spun themselves around my face, over things that crunched and crumbled under my feet.

The corridor ended at stairs and what seemed to be a barless cell. I cupped my hand around another match and saw a rusted piece of pipe with a shower head still attached. This had been a small bathroom. There was little left now but the gratings in the floor. The outside wall had partially collapsed. That was where the glow had come from. The night outside was lighter than the deep darkness inside these thick, barred walls. The free, wonderful outside!

I picked up the piece of pipe and weighed it in my hand. It was heavy as lead. It probably was lead. Then I scrambled over the crumbled wall.

In a second I saw the sky, bright with stars between patches of cloud, the path, and Priest. His back was to me as he sat at the edge of the path, looking down over the drop below to the bend where Maxie and Cowboy would reappear, maybe had reappeared already. Music thumped softly from the black box beside him. The lantern was off, set close to his right hand.

I tightened my grip on the pipe and crept up behind him. I'd promised myself what I would do to this fat little creep when I got the chance, and now I had the chance. I stood behind Priest's unsuspecting back with the pipe raised, and I thought about Biddy and me and what was at stake, and I brought the pipe down on the back of his head.

He fell forward, rolling down the steep, grassy slope, coming to a stop by a stubby bush. I scrambled after him. I should hit him again, I knew, because I hadn't hit him hard enough the first time, and he was moving. He shook his head from side to side as if he were dazed. Cripes! He might even get up. But I couldn't hit him again. It just wasn't in me. He was lying on his back, groaning, so I rolled him over on the mound of his stomach. Then I yanked the string from my hood, pulled his wrists behind him, and tied them tight.

"What you doin'?" he muttered. "Who's this?"

"Shut up," I said. I fished the ice pick from his pocket and slid it into mine.

It wasn't easy getting Priest's belt from around the top of his black pants. I had to half lift him to pull it free from the front loops, and he felt as if he weighed three hundred pounds. I straddled his legs while I drew the belt tight around his ankles

No kidding, that belt was long enough to circle the waist of a small elephant.

His glasses had slipped down on one ear, so I threw them away into the long grass. Without them he couldn't go anywhere. I should gag him too, I knew, in case he yelled. But I'd have to be super careful. A gag has to be placed just right or it can choke a person. I pulled off one of his cruddy shoes and took the sock from his foot. Pee-ew! The sock stretched enough for me to knot it behind his head. It wasn't as tight as it should be, but it would take Priest a while to wiggle it loose. As soon as I straightened, I saw Cowboy and Maxie coming up the path. No flashlight. The battery must have died out completely by now.

The two of them were already at the second bend, and moving at a fast clip. I looked at them and I knew it was decision time. I could race back to the cell block, pull the lever, and let Biddy out. Together we could try to make it around them and down to the ranger hut. But they'd still be free and able to chase us, maybe get us and Maybelline, too.

The other thing I could do was hide here till they passed, sitting on Priest's fat head the way I'd sat on his brother's, ten lifetimes ago. Then I could beat it to the ranger station myself. But what about Biddy? Cowboy and Maxie would have time to get to her. They'd find me gone and they'd drag her out of the cell, take her with them as a hostage or worse. Or ... I could ... That "or" made me sweat, crouched there in the cold night air.

I breathed hard, watching them. Cowboy's poncho swung savagely as he loped along with his long-legged stride. He looked as if he were ready to explode. Beside him, Maxie danced and pranced, leaping along like a crazy gazelle.

That was when I made my decision. It was going to be the "or." I wanted to get the two of them myself.

CHAPTER

12

The lantern and radio were where Priest had left them, when he'd fallen forward. I threw the radio down the hill away from him, picked up the lantern, and switched it off. I carried it and the piece of lead piping with me as I climbed across the jumble of bricks into the shower room. Then I turned the corner into Broadway.

I stood close to the cell door levers and tried to think what would happen next. First, Cowboy and Maxie would see Priest wasn't where he should be. They'd think he was inside, hassling me and Biddy, or that he'd gotten bored and wandered off. I hadn't time to think past that because I suddenly heard the two of them.

Cowboy's voice was tight with rage. He turned with his back to the cell block. "Priest! Where are you?"

"Priest!" Maxie's voice yodelled down the echoing aisle, repeating and repeating into the distance. "Hey!" he said. "It's like in a cave."

"He's gone," Cowboy spat. "And he's taken the light with him. What's wrong with you guys? Can't you do anything you're told? First Bean — then him. When he gets back, so help me . . ."

"Hey! I did what you told me! I went with you, didn't I?"

I stood well back, able to hear them but not see them unless I stepped forward. And I tightened my grip on the pipe.

"I'm going down now to get that lying kid," Cowboy said. "Open the door when I tell you, and close it fast as soon as I'm inside. I don't want the girl running. And I plan on being in there with Danny-Boy a long while."

The last words drifted back to me along with the clump of Cowboy's boots on the hard, stone floor.

"What's this?" The clumping stopped, and his voice echoed back. "That idiot Priest's been playing with paper airplanes again. The place is littered with them."

Close to me, very close, Maxie giggled. He was at the levers, shuffling around, his feet tapping, all of him humming like a generator under full power.

Cowboy's footsteps stopped. I imagined him peering into the blackness of the cell, steaming to get at me.

I heard Biddy beg, "Please don't hurt him, Cowboy. He's just a kid. He was only trying to save us." Good old Biddy, knowing I was out, smart enough to play along.

"You! Ranger!" Cowboy said. "Maxie's at one end of the cell block and Priest's at the other. So don't even try to run when these doors open."

His voice bellowed down Broadway. "Now!" and the echoes, "Now, now, now," recoiled from the towering walls and ceilings.

I stepped forward on the balls of my feet and saw the shadow that was Maxie pull down the big metal lever. The doors clanged open.

"Close them," Cowboy yelled and I knew he was in the dark of my empty cell, reaching out to find me.

While the clatter of the doors smashing shut was still ringing in the air, I made my move. I had one chance to get it right, and only one. Maxie wasn't Priest. He wouldn't tumble and roll. If I missed the first time, he'd be on me, and Biddy and I would both be finished. I stretched the way a tennis pro stretches to serve a smashing, cannonball serve. I brought the pipe down the way the pro brings down the racquet. My breath came out in a tennis pro grunt. If I'd hit Maxie's head I'd have pulped his skull. But something, some reflex between my brain and my hand changed my aim from head to shoulder.

Maxie sank with a sag of the knees. His shadowy hand dragged at the lever and I was terrified that his weight would pull on it and open the doors again. But then his hand slid down to join the rest of him on the floor.

"The kid's not here! Open the doors!" Cowboy's voice screamed up the aisle. There was a string of shouted curses, and he rattled the bars. Biddy called my name.

I didn't answer right away. Instead I bent over Maxie, away from the stretch of his long arms, and turned the lantern full on him. One hand came up against the light and his legs fluttered. I swear, Maxie would be squirming on the table if he were having open heart surgery.

I turned the light on the number of the cell closest to him. Then I ran back to the lever and opened the door to that cell.

Cowboy and Biddy were still yelling and I called to her. "It's okay. Everything's under control." At the same time I took Maxie's legs and began to drag him toward the cell.

It's good to be small when you're trying to crawl through a mouse hole. It's not so great when you're pulling a weight like Maxie. He's skinny, but there's a lot of weight in those long bones. I thought of letting Biddy out to help me, but there was something in me that wanted to finish this alone.

Maxie jerked and flapped like a beached fish as I tugged him through the cell door. His long hair trailed behind him, brushing its own path through the dirt of ages on the floor. It was the last part of him to clear the door space.

I ran back and closed the cell. Then I leaned against the door of the old shower room, my knees shaking and my heart sounding like a locomotive.

Biddy and Cowboy were quiet now. Around me the ghost prison held its breath, listening. From outside came a chirping that wasn't from crickets. I recognized Priest's weak little voice. "Help, somebody! Help!"

I had them all . . . all four of them. Jelly Bean and Priest outside. Cowboy and Maxie trapped in the cages. I'd done it. Me, little Danny Sullivan, nonbrave, noneverything. There should have been cheers and bugles playing. But there was only silence.

I turned off the light and began to walk along the darkness of Broadway, swinging the unlit lantern in one hand and my piece of lead pipe in the other. My feet fluttered Priest's little airplanes, puffing them across the floor. I felt unreal. I had a sudden vision of me and the cells and the island. I was way up above, looking down, seeing no color except tones of black and gray and lighter gray.

From my perch I could make out the flat detail of the exercise yard and the old parade ground. The derelict houses. The chimneys and lighthouse pointing to the black sky. The flat roofs of the prison. And me, walking along the straightness between the cells, the only thing moving on that cold gray rock that rose mysteriously from that cold gray sea. How did it get here? How did I?

Biddy reached her arms through the bars. I saw their dark outline and I set down the lantern and pipe and squeezed her hands. My hands hurt.

"Did you get Maxie?"

I nodded, though I wasn't sure she could see.

"And Priest?" I nodded again.

"Aren't you going to let me out, Danny?" She was crying and I had a hard time answering because I was crying, too.

"I'll let you out right now," I said. "First I need to get your cell number, though. I don't want to let *him* out instead."

"We'll go down to Maybelline and she'll . . ."

"You'll have to go alone for Maybelline," I whispered. "I'll stay. Remember the hole in the back wall? I think it's too small for him, but who knows. I'll keep guard."

She turned her face against my hand. The salt of her tears stung the raw places.

I picked up the lantern and pipe and turned the light into my cell. *My* cell? When did it get to be mine?

Cowboy stood, stiff and silent in the middle of the cage. The big hat shrouded his face and the poncho hung motionless. His feet were planted wide apart. He could have been a figure in the wax museum on the Wharf — "Portrait of a Gun Slinger. Wanted dead or alive."

The light shone in his eyes, making them gleam the way the cat's eyes had gleamed. I realized that he hadn't said anything while I'd talked with Biddy. Somehow that made him more sinister. I stood way back and I knew I was still scared of him.

Something moved under the shadow of the hat and I stared, not believing. Cowboy was smiling. "It's not over, Danny-Boy," he said then. "We'll all be going back to the city. They'll have nothing to hold us on. We'll be on the streets again . . . and in school. You'd better run far and fast, Danny-Boy. And you'd better keep running."

"This time I'll testify," I said.

Biddy spoke quickly. "I will, too. How about assault with a deadly weapon? Kidnapping. Attempted murder."

"Trespassing?" Cowboy was amused.

"That too."

I wish I could say that I wasn't afraid anymore and that I never would be again. But I was. I held the lantern with both hands to keep it from shaking.

Cowboy's smile widened. "You've got no guts, you know, Danny-Boy."

"Neither have you." I saw suddenly and clearly what I'd never seen before. I knew why I hadn't hit Priest harder and why I hadn't smashed in Maxie's head.

"Liking to hurt and scare doesn't make you a hero, Cowboy," I said. "No way."

"And what does, kid?"

"I don't know. Maybe being afraid, and doing what you have to do anyway."

Cowboy was still smiling as I walked down Broadway to pull the lever and set Biddy free.

They sent a coast guard boat for us when Maybelline phoned. It came out of the darkness that lay between the city and Alcatraz, its big light like a yellow eye, searching us out.

Jelly Bean was brought on board on a stretcher. Cowboy and Priest and Maxie followed him; all three were handcuffed. I thought maybe they wouldn't look at me, but they did. It will be a while before I forget those looks. It will be forever before I forget the way Cowboy tipped his hat despite the handcuffs.

Biddy and I stood at the stern as the boat pulled away from the island. Maybelline was on the dock with Shadow Cat in her arms. When she waved,

Shadow seized his chance to jump free, stalking from the fall of lamplight into the darkness that was Alcatraz.

I huddled small inside my red jacket.

"Are you okay?" Biddy put her arm through mine and squeezed.

"Sure."

"What are you thinking?"

"That I'll be walking along Geary someday, or maybe Van Ness, and I'll look up and see Cowboy. And he'll still be smiling."

"He won't be walking anywhere, Danny. This time there'll be two of us to testify against the Outlaws. They won't get out of this."

I stared across the churn of water. Biddy didn't know the Outlaws the way I knew them.

Her voice was soft. "If you *do* see him . . . it's not going to happen, but if you do . . . you won't run, will you, Danny?"

I couldn't stop shivering. "I don't think so. I've been telling myself I won't. But how can I be sure until it happens?"

We stood in silence. The island had almost disappeared now, hiding itself between sea and sky, pulling its mists around it. I turned my back and faced the beauty of the city.